CALLED TO DUTY
BOOK 2 – PAYING THE PIPER

Doug Murray

CALLED TO DUTY
BOOK 2 – PAYING THE PIPER

DOUBLE DRAGON

PROLOGUE

Mukalla, Yemen...

Jamil Khaldun shook with fear as three armed men led him away from his home. "What have I done?" He asked them, voice high and pleading. "I am a loyal Muslim!"

"You are a traitor to the faith." The answer came from the third of the armed men—the one who was clearly their leader. "You have betrayed your people to the enemy—to the infidels of the great Satan."

"You are wrong! I would never..." Jamil stopped as three more armed men appeared from another house, another prisoner in their midst.

They have Murad Hayyan! Jamil's eyes widened as he saw his friend led down the street. They know! But How? We were promised that everything would be safe, secret...

"You understand now," the leader nodded slowly as he watched Jamil's face. "We have the truth of it. You and that one," he indicated Murad. "Provided the information that led to the death of Nasir Wahishi." His eyes bored into Jamil's. "You are a spy for the forever damned CIA!"

"But..." Jamil sputtered, knowing in his heart of heart that he had been betrayed and would soon be.

"Bring them," the leader ordered, turning away. "We will show them the wrath of Allah!"

A hard hand pushed Jamil forward and he stumbled along behind the leader, mind racing. But how can they know? How is it possible? Jamil shook his head sadly, realizing that he would never know the truth.

He began to pray--for his soul and the lives of his family.

"This will do," the leader called out a few minutes later. "Have them kneel there," he pointed toward the beach overlooking the Gulf of Aden. "We will let the sea drink their blood."

"I am innocent!" Jamil cried out. "I have done nothing!"

"If that is true," the leader sneered. "Then Allah will save you. However," he looked up, searching the bright blue sky above. "I see no sign of that." He brought his gaze down to Jamil. "Do you?"

"I tell you I am a true son of Allah!" The same merciless hand pressed Jamil's shoulders downward, forcing his head lower until his face inches from the shifting waters.

"I am innocent!" Jamil cried, fighting against the pressure holding him down—but he had no chance. No chance at all.

"If we have wronged you," the leader told him. "Then we will certainly apologize when we meet in Paradise, if not…" He shrugged.

Jamil tried to stand up, tried to get away the hand that held him helpless while Murad was forced to kneel at his side. He was still arguing with the leader when he felt a metallic object touch the back of the head.

"Allah help me!" He cried just before he heard a sound like thunder and felt a dull pain that pushed his head forward into eternal darkness.

CHAPTER ONE

"How's it going, Sean?" Frank Farrell, just back from another in an endless series of meetings peered into his protégé's office. "Did you finish that Math assignment?"

"Hours ago," Sean Piper, having just turned nineteen years of age, was taking online courses through the University of Virginia. It was the only way his mother would allow him to work for Farrell in the older man's very special organization that was an odd hybrid sibling of the CIA and Homeland Security.

"Did the History and English too." He nodded toward his computer and changed the subject as he pulled up an image. "Did you see this?"

"I doubt it," Farrell moved furthers into the room, walking around Sean's desk so he could look at the indicated monitor. "I've been in budget meetings all morning."

"Wire services picked this up an hour or two ago." The youngster enlarged the image until it filled the monitor. "It was broadcast by Al Qaeda in Yemen. They're saying that these two men were spies responsible for the death of Nasir Wahishi." Sean glanced at his partner and boss. "Isn't that the bigshot they hit with a drone strike? The one the President's been patting himself on the back over?"

"Nasir Wahishi," Farrell nodded. "Al Qaeda's No. 2 leader worldwide and head of the organization's franchise in Yemen." He leaned closer to the screen, a worried look crossing his face. "Can you give me a better look at their faces?"

"Maybe," Sean tapped on his keyboard. "It'll lose some clarity."

"Do what you can."

"Okay," the youngster hit 'enter' and watched the image expand. "Good enough?"

"My God!" Farrell leaned closer. "It is!" He pointed to one of the men sprawled in the sand. "That's Jamil Khaldun!" He shook his head. "I wonder…"

"Someone you knew?"

"Show me the other man," Farrell ignored the question, biting on his lip as he studied the screen. "Please!"

Sean shifted the images, pushing the other kneeling man to the center of the screen.

"Murad Hayyan!" Farrell stared at the screen. "Both of them! But how could they know?" He looked toward Sean, eyes stricken. "How could they possibly know?"

"Know what?"

"Know that these two men," Farrell nodded at the screen. "Were our best agents in Yemen." He ran a hand across his eyes. "Their identities were supposed to be top secret!"

"Somebody must have talked."

"Impossible." Farrell shook his head. "No one in Yemen knew! The information was kept as need-to-know file at Langley. Unless the CIA's been penetrated…"

"Maybe it has," Sean interjected, returning his attention to the keyboard. "You know about the

8

hack that got into the files of the Office of Personnel Management?"

"What does that have to do with anything?" Farrell snorted. "That was just another Chinese cyber-attack, wasn't it?"

"That's what the Administration has been telling the media," Sean pulled up a news stories about the hack. "They say that the hackers got full information packages on at least twenty million government employees," he looked at his partner. "And I'm pretty sure the real number is a lot higher!"

"But the records of CIA personnel and those working for the agency in foreign countries aren't kept with the OPM's files."

"Maybe not," Sean scratched his chin, half-smiling as he felt the stubble now growing there (he had always been told he was 'baby-faced', now maybe he could get people to admit he was a man!). "But it might be possible to get from the OPM system into the DOD," he looked at Farrell. "Or the CIA."

"Find out." Farrell came to a quick decision. "I'll call Mary Max—we're going to have to talk about this!" He shook his head. "Soon!"

***

NEW YORK CITY—THE CORNER OF FIFTH AVE AND EIGHTH STREET

Harold Carter—formerly Hamid Kalid—smiled as a new rider slipped into the back seat of his cab. He loved the city this time of year. The springtime air was just warm enough to allow him to keep his windows open but not yet so warm that he would be forced to turn on his air conditioner.

Harold knew all about heat, he'd grown up in Iraq where it was warm all year around (except for a week or so in January) and devices such as air conditioners were only for the rich and politically connected.

Harold had not been a member of that group. He'd been nothing more than one of millions of poor Sunni—and, like many of them, a common laborer.

When the Americans came, he had seen a chance to change his lot in life and had gone to work for them. He had been instrumental in helping them find the people and weapons they were seeking and made himself useful in other ways.

He became 'important'.

So much so that when the Americans left Iraq, his 'handler' arranged for him to come with them and, with the help of his superiors in the CIA—gave Hamid a new identity—and a job!

True, it wasn't an 'important' job. In fact, it was rather menial.

But Harold (he made sure to always think of himself as such) enjoyed driving a cab. It gave him a great deal of freedom and allowed him to see every corner of this great city.

Today he was working in and around Greenwich Village, a place where he always found interesting fares.

Like the one climbing aboard now.

"Welcome sir!" Harold's English was quite good by this time. "Where do you want to go?"

"Downtown," the man growled, not looking in Harold's direction. "Pier 92."

"Pier 92." Harold nodded and started his meter, puzzled by the destination. The clubs there don't open for hours, he knew. And there's nothing else there. He glanced into the mirror. But the customer is always right, so, he shrugged. Off we go!

He put the cab into gear and pulled into traffic, cutting off another cab which honked in anger— which Harold, like any other New York driver, ignored.

Traffic was heavy and it took nearly thirty minutes to get all the way downtown but Harold finally pulled up at the Pier in question and flipped the flag down. "This is it, sir." He looked at the meter. "That will be $51."

"Good," the man in the back of the cab opened the door and stepped out.

"Sir!" Harold rolled down the passenger-side window and leaned out. "The fare sir!"

The man smiled a hard smile and reached under his lightweight jacket, producing a large-caliber handgun. "It is you who will pay the fare, traitor!" He leaned forward, the muzzle of the weapon trained on Harold's forehead. "Open the front door."

Harold did as he was told and watched as the man re-entered the cab, sliding into the front seat where there was no pane of bullet-proof to protect Harold from the pistol that never wavered.

"Now," the man smiled. "Let us drive a little way down the pier."

11

Harold nodded, knowing what was to come—and seeing no way to avoid it.

He said a prayer and put the cab into gear, driving in the direction indicated.

***

"Did you see this?" Sean asked as Farrell entered the office the next morning. "Somebody got beheaded in New York!"

"Some Muslim thing?" The older man headed toward his own desk, pulling off his jacket as he went. "Maybe one of those ISIS wannabes we've been hearing about?"

"Maybe—the cops haven't said anything left."

"Who was killed?"

"A cabbie—name of Carter."

Farrell froze in place, jacket still over one shoulder. "Not Harold Carter."

"That's right," Sean nodded. "Harold Carter." He looked at his partner. "Did you know him?"

"His real name was Hamid Kalid." Farrell pulled his jacket back on. "And we've definitely got a problem." He gestured to his partner. "Come one—we've got to see Mary Max right now!"

***

"You're sure the murdered individuals were CIA assets?" Mary Max Holston had just started drinking her first cup of office coffee when Farrell came knocking on her door. "I mean, the Agency hasn't raised any red flags that I know about."

"They may not have noticed," Farrell plopped into a seat across from his boss, waving Sean to another chair at his side. "I'm sure someone is taking a look at the killings in Yemen, but unless

12

they know enough to check the confidential files, they'll find nothing to be concerned about."

"Check with them," Mary Max nodded slowly. "And make a visit to the FBI cyber unit—see how sure they are that the Chinese hacked OPM."

"OPM and CIA aren't connected…"

"Then see if anyone else hit one of the government firewalls." She looked into Farrell's face. "Sean can check on that—it's his specialty," she glanced at the younger man. "It is, isn't it?"

The youngster nodded. "I may be able to find some evidence of a break-in." He shrugged. "I'm going to have to have access to the raw data to be sure."

"The FBI guys will give it to you—if they give you a hard time, give me a call," Mary Max smiled a dangerous smile. "I'll take care of it."

Sean nodded.

"Okay, both of you get on it." Mary Max made a shooing motion with her hand. "Find out what's really going on and see me later this afternoon." She took a sip from her cup--and made a face. "And bring some decent coffee with you."

"Yes Ma'am!" Farrell stood up and headed for the door, Sean just a step behind him.

***

"Aren't you a little young to be an agent of…" James Tarver looked at the ID card presented to him. "Homeland Security?"

"Yes," Sean answered. "Yes I am." He smiled. "Is that going to be a problem?"

"I guess not," Tarver handed the ID card back, eyes wary. "So Mr. Piper," he frowned and held out a hand. "What do you want from us?"

13

"Your people discovered the hack into OPM, right?" Sean asked him.

"So?"

"I'd like to look at the raw data that allowed you to trace the hack to the Chinese." He looked the FBI man in the eye. "We suspect that another hack was piggy-backed on the one you caught."

"You're saying we missed something?"

"I'm saying that it looks as if another agency was hacked at the same time." He bit into his lower lip. "I think that's too much of coincidence to be random—which tells me that the two acts are related."

"Impossible." Tarver shook his head. "My people would have detected a second entry."

"Would they?" Sean leaned forward, eyes mild as he raised an eyebrow. "Or would they have stopped when they found the initial, large intrusion, assuming that it was the only one."

"You don't think too much of my people, do you?"

"I don't know your people, sir." Sean shook his head. "I do know that there was almost certainly a second hack—and I need to find where it came from."

"No." Tarver shook his head. "I don't want you conducting that kind of investigation. My people would feel slighted, distrusted..."

"This is important! And I have no intention of slighting your people."

"I said no." Tarver glared at the younger man. "And that's my final word."

"All right," Sean pulled out his cell phone. "I'll have to report this to my boss. She said to call her if there was any sort of problem."

Tarver frowned. "Your boss?"

"Ms. Holston." Sean cradled the phone in his left hand and unlocked the keypad with his right.

"Mary Max Holston?"

"Yeah," Sean looked at the other agent. "Why?"

"Don't call her." Tarver made a negating motion with his hand. "I really don't want any trouble with Mary Max!"

"You know her?"

"Everyone in the intelligence community knows Mary Max Holston." He looked at Sean. "Okay—come on in, I'll give you access to the data you want." He shook his head. "We'll use my office. If I'm lucky, nobody will notice…"

So everyone knows Mary Max, Sean thought, putting his phone away. I'm going to have to get Frank to tell me just why that's the case. He smiled. And if he won't tell me, I might just have to hack into her file and find out for myself. He watched Agent Tarver punched a code into the keypad alongside the door.

1-2-3-4, Sean shook his head. And this guy is in charge of the FBI Cyber office! He followed Tarver through the door. No wonder the Chinese keep hacking into our government databases without any trouble!

Sean had watched a few episodes of CSI: CYBER, the television series that was supposed to be about the team of FBI agents in the room beyond the just unlocked-door. He'd thought it a bit farfetched but now, looking over the handful of men and women slouching in front of government-issue consoles, he realized that it was utter bullshit.

"This way," Tarver motioned him to the far side of the room. "My office is over here."

Sean followed the older man, taking in the ambience of the room around him. Unlike the TV show's headquarters, this room had no large screens, no central 'hub'. It was nothing more than a standard government office--eight desks in two rows that were lined up parallel to the outside wall. The windows were covered with black venetian blinds to make the screens easier to read—which left only desk lamps and a single, rather dim, overhead fluorescent as the only illumination in the room.

The desks were olive-drab metallic hulks— Government Issue taken from one of the warehouse scattered around the District. Each desk had a blotter (green, of course) and a desktop computer built to government specifications—which meant it was bigger, heavier, and less powerful than the average civilian tablet.

"What kind of internet connection do you have?" Sean asked as he stepped into Tarver's office.

"Standard set-up," Tarver gestured the youngster to his desk. "The whole building is wired for Wi-Fi. We just log on."

"How fast?"

"I don't know," Tarver shrugged. "Maybe 250 or 300 mbps on average."

Sean tried to keep his disbelief from showing. His own office computer was plugged into a T-1 line and got more than 5 million mbps.

I guess Mary Max really did right by me, he told himself, sitting in Tarver's seat. Way better than their boss did for these guys!

He woke the desktop up.

"You want to put in the password," he asked Tarver.

"Go right ahead and do it for me," Tarver settled into a chair in the corner of the room. "ID is JIMBOT and the password is 11-12-75."

"Your birthday?"

Tarver shrugged.

"Okay," Sean entered the ID and password, nodding as the computer came to life.

"File marked OPM has all the date on the hack—help yourself."

"Thanks," Sean opened the file in question and began going through the information, searching for the incursion in question.

It didn't take long to find it.

"I see that they got in through a desktop in the accounting office," Sean began searching for the computer that had perpetrated the attack. "This got bounced around a little…" He followed the IP address from country to country, following it back to its point of origin. "They weren't too serious about this—guess they figured they'd be safe enough since they were doing the hack on orders."

"That's what we figured."

"There's a branch point here," Sean froze the data. "Another NIC address appears for a moment."

"We assumed that was just an artefact—a network error."

"Maybe," Sean looked at the NIC address, tracked it back to its IP. "Hong Kong." He muttered, looking at the information in front of him. "That's interesting." He packaged that segment of data and e-mailed it to his office computer, securing it with a password and cipher.

"Find what you wanted?"

"Maybe." Sean stood up. "I'll have to go into this a little deeper, but I can do that from my own office." He put out his hand. "Thanks for the co-operation."

"No sweat," Tarver grinned, showing a mouthful of bright white teeth arrayed around a single gold one. "Give Mary Max my best."

"Will do." Sean nodded. "And if there's ever anything I can do for you…"

"I'll give a call." Tarver held the door open, hurrying the young agent out of his office. "You have my word on that."

Sean nodded and scanned the drab 'government Issue' office spread out around him. I could help them with a lot of things, he thought making his way toward the outer door. But they wouldn't thank me for it.

A moment later he was in the hall and heading for his own office in the taller half of the J. Edgar Hoover building.

CHAPTER TWO

"Frank Farrell!" The heavily-tanned man smiled as Farrell stepped into his office. "Son of a bitch!"

"Good to see you, Adam." Farrell took the other man's hand and gave it a firm shake. "How's business here at the Company?"

"Same old, same old." Adam Malin had been recruited into the CIA by one of his college professors (after he started sleeping with her). His language and organizational skills made him a very successful analyst and now, nearly twenty years later, he was running the 'Iraq, Iran, Lebanon, and Syria Intelligence Desk,' the hottest seat in the intelligence section since the rise of ISIS. "What's an old reprobate like you doing out here?"

"Got a couple of questions," Farrell sat down and produced a tablet which he keyed to 'ON'. "Have you seen these?" He handed the device to Malin and watched his face as he looked at the first headline.

"I wasn't aware of this." He moved to the next screen, his lip compressing as he saw the name there. "Howard Carter." He shook his head. "I remember him from the days when he was Hamid Kalid--a nice guy—we brought him back to the States when things got to warm out in the sandbox-- got him a job..." He shook his head and stared at the newspaper report. "Driving a cab!"

"We think that somebody got into your files—pulled data about people we recruited in various countries."

"Our files are secure!"

"Are you sure?" Farrell raised an eyebrow. "Because this sure looks as if someone got in."

"Frank, we change passwords every week, check the firewall every other day…"

"We think someone piggy-backed on the Chinese hack of OPM and got in that way." Farrell leaned forward. "Is that possible?"

"I'm not sure…" Malin tapped a finger on his desk. "I wouldn't think so, but there are so many things those computer guys can do…"

"Check it for me." Farrell looked at his friend. "As quickly as you can."

"I'll call our IT people; they can do a quick scrub of the system."

"I'll wait." Farrell sank back into his chair. "Mary Max wants us to give her a full briefing this afternoon."

"You're working for Mary Max?" Malin picked up the phone on his desk and punched in a 3-digit extension. "I thought she got out of the business?" He looked at his friend. "For that matter, I thought you got out too!"

"We both did." Farrell smiled and shrugged. "Before we came back."

"Good thing," Malin shook his head. "We need people like you."

"People like us."

"I don't know, Frank. It seems like…" He held up a finger and turned his attention to the phone. "Lou? I need you to run a check," Malin sighed. "Yeah, right now! You're looking for an incursion into asset files." He looked at the tablet. "Mid-East—past ten years or so." Malin listened for a moment. "Okay, bring the results to my office as soon as you're done and Lou," his eyes met Farrell's. "This is to be treated as 'Need to Know'—my eyes only—got it?" He nodded once. "Good, see you soon."

He put the phone down and stared at the tablet. "Okay, Frank—what do you think is going on…?"

***

Imam Aaban Saadeh smiled as he read a chapter from the Qur'an. The mosque was doing well, with a solid group of the faithful coming to pray several times each day.

Saadeh had been doubtful about the possibility of building a congregation here in the United States, but he had learned that American Muslims were just as devout as those in Iran—and far less likely to do violence to members of other sects.

They are good people, he thought as he watched his flock begin their rakats of prayer, the most puritan and devout counted each prayer on their fingertips only, the others used the more common prayer beads. I have been very fortunate…

Even as the thought crossed his mind, the outer door banged open, drawing all eyes toward it. They saw a tall man with a dark beard strode across the floor, ignoring them as he bore down on the Imam.

"You are Aaban Saadeh?" He intoned.

"Yes," the Imam answered, frowning. "What can I do for you?"

21

"You can burn in Jahannam!" The man drew a pistol from beneath his shirt and fired three shots at Aaban, hitting him in the chest and groin.

The Imam dropped to the floor, moaning.

"This man is a traitor to the true faith!" The man looked at the stunned congregants, the pistol held above his head. "He has given aid to the Infidel and he must pay." The dark man took a long step toward the fallen Imam and pointed the pistol toward the supine man's head.

"Wait..." Aaban whispered. "I did not..."

"Allahu Ackbar!" The tall man shouted—and pulled the trigger.

Aaban Saadeh's congregation watched, mouths agape, as the man fired a second shot into their Imam's skull before turning on his heel and calmly walking across the floor and out the door.

***

"There's no question someone hacked into the CIA data base—they accessed the master payment files where the records of everyone that's gotten money from the Agency are kept." Sean shook his head as he thought about the extent of the. "I found an IP address that was different from the one the Chinese military hackers used—one that traced back to Hong Kong," he dropped a tablet with the appropriate information onto Mary Max's desk. "I also found enough traces to convince me that whoever did the hack used a vulnerability scanner on the OPM server although I wouldn't have thought that would be enough..." He shrugged. "I'll know more when I have time to get further into it."

"What's a 'vulnerability scanner?" Mary Max asked, taking a large cup of coffee from Farrell.

"It's a tool used to quickly check computers on a network for known weaknesses." Sean told her. "It's a bit more versatile than a port scanner which checks to see which ports on a specified computer are "open" or available for access." He shook his head. "Considering the kinds of passwords in use around here, any reasonably competent hacker could get in without any trouble at all."

"What makes you say that?" Farrell asked, returning to his seat.

"I was at the FBI's 'Cyber' division checking on their data dump of the Chinese incursion." Sean smiled. "They seem to have tremendous respect for you, ma'am—at least they gave me what I wanted when I used your name."

"Nice to know."

"Passwords?" Farrell repeated.

"Oh—well the Agent-in-charge of the Cyber division let me into their offices through a coded access door." He looked at Farrell. "The password was 1-2-3-4."

Farrell sighed.

"Worse," Sean continued. "The agent's own computer's password was his birthday—and his ID was just a variant on his name." The youngster shook his head. "Not very secure."

"We've got to do something about that!" Mary Max said, making a note. "The President's people keep talking about how important cyber security is but they keep pushing any real rule changes further and further into the future." She shook her head. "I'll talk to Steff, maybe she can talk somebody over there into actually getting off their ass and doing something now!"

She tapped her pen on the desk for a moment, and then turned to the young agent, the barest hint of a smile on her lips. "You said you traced the hack to Hong Kong?"

"Yes Ma'am," Sean leaned forward. "The main attack—the one on OPM--definitely came from China—probably from one of their military hacking units, but there was a secondary incursion—it came at almost the same time and was aimed at the CIA system." He shook his head. "I think it might have gone through a financial port..."

"CIA agents get paid through the government payroll system," Farrell put in. "Their salary and tax records are kept in the OPM system which is far less secure than the Company's own network." He frowned. "But I thought that there was a confidential paymaster set-up for non-government employees."

Sean wasn't paying attention. Instead, he was looking at his tablet. He'd set up a series of search parameters that were to pass reports of violent deaths of a certain type to him.

One had just been registered.

"Frank," he passed the tablet to his partner. "Do you know someone named 'Aaban Saadeh?"

"Crap!" Farrell stared at the report on the recent shooting for a long second, than shook his head and handed the tablet back to Sean.

"I gather that you do?" Mary Max put in.

"He was an Iranian Imam who gave us access to information about their atomic programs." Farrell gestured as he looked at his boss. "We got him out of the country more than three years ago and set him up in a Mosque right here in the District."

"15th Street." Sean read from the tablet. "Near the Bladensburg Pike."

Farrell nodded slowly. "It's too bad--he was a good man..."

"He was shot four times—in front of his congregation," Sean read the police report. "The shooter called him a 'Traitor to the true faith.'"

"We can't let this go on," Farrell said. "We promised these people safety. Gave our words that their identities would remain unknown!"

"How many are there?"

"I don't know," Farrell made a throw-away gesture. "Hundreds?"

"Too many to guard," Mary Max looked at the two men in front of her. "It's going to be up to you two to find out who has the information and cut it off at the source."

"The CIA..."

"Cannot be trusted until they fix the leak in their security system." Mary Max shook her head. "No. This is exactly the kind of thing we were created to handle." She looked at Farrell. "Of course, if you don't think you're up to it..."

"Of course we're up to it." Farrell looked at his partner. "The only question is—can we stop it before any more good people are killed?"

"Do your best." Mary Max told them flatly, her eyes on Farrell. "Even if that means going to Hong Kong."

"You know it will," Farrell sighed. "At least for openers."

"Am I missing something?"

"Ask your partner," Mary Max nodded toward Farrell. "He'll fill you in on everything you need to know." She smiled. "And if he doesn't, come back and ask me."

Farrell glared at her as he led Sean out of the room.

CHAPTER THREE

Twelve hours later, they were airborne—on their way to Hong Kong.

"I could get used to this!" Sean said as he stretched out in one of the very plush seats mounted on either side of the Gulfstream GV's interior.

"Mary Max must have pulled some strings," Farrell noted, relaxing in his own seat. "I figured we'd end up going commercial for sure."

"She's worried."

"She should be," Farrell reclined his seat and put his feet on the rest that appeared in front of him. "If we can't protect our assets, nobody will trust us and vital sources of Intel will dry up and disappear." He sat up a little, looked at his partner. "You told Lisa—your mother—that we were heading out of town, right?"

"I did." Sean nodded. "She said to give you her love and ask when you're going to come and visit her again."

"Well," Farrell's face colored a bit. "That kind of depends…"

"On me?" Sean smiled. "No worries on my end! If you can make Mom happy, it's fine with me!"

"We'll talk about that later!" Farrell turned away, leaning back in his seat. "For now, it'd be smart to get some sleep—it's a long flight."

"Before I do that," Sean stared at his partner. "Tell me about Hong Kong."

"Can't it wait?"

"No." Sean shook his head. "It can't."

Farrell sighed. "Okay," he sat back up, looking at the younger man. "The Company station chief in Hong Kong is one Brian Kelly, known to one and all as 'Captain Kek'."

"Captain Kek?"

"It's a nickname he got in elementary school— seems he was a hall monitor, one so annoying that some of the other kids began to pass around notes saying, 'Kill Captain Kelly' which became 'KEK'." Farrell shook his head. "The name stuck."

"I'll bet I could guess what his computer password would be!"

"Don't underestimate Kelly—he's a smart man—and really good with high-tech stuff. When we were testing drones in Iraq and Afghanistan, he was the main pilot on most of the flights."

"So what's the problem between the two of you?"

"During the Libyan fiasco, he was my backup—in command of the annex where the rest of our shooters were stationed. When things went belly-up and the higher-ups ordered us to stand down..." He looked at Sean, pain in his eyes. "Stand down even though that would mean the death of a dozen of our people—including your father." Farrell bit into his lower lip. "Kek didn't protest or argue with our masters. Instead, he just saluted and did what he was told. He kept his shooters in the annex, sitting on their hands while the rest of our people get slaughtered." He shook his head. "I've never forgiven him for that."

"That's interesting." Sean leaned forward. "I didn't see his name on the official report."

"That report is Top Secret! How could you…"

Sean tapped his laptop. "The passwords used by the National Archive are even worse than the ones used by the FBI."

"Then you know what I did…."

"I've known for a while," Sean made a tiny gesture with his hand. "Long before I met Doctor Ramnarain and his merry band."

"And yet you agreed to work with me anyway!"

"Frank," Sean looked his partner in the eye. "I've seen the reports. I know that you did all that you could possibly do to help my father." He raised an eyebrow. "I also know that you quit the CIA because of what the men above you did—or refused to do." He held out a hand. "How could I possibly blame you for what happened?"

"Thanks." Farrell nodded once. "That means a lot."

"No problem." Sean grinned. "Look at it this way--you got me a good job—a job with a future," he looked at Farrell. "With a partner I trust."

Farrell nodded again.

"Now let's both get some sleep," Sean yawned. "I have it on good authority that this is a long flight."

The two of them stretched out in their seats and, a few minutes later, filled the cabin with quiet snoring.

***

Hong Kong ('Fragrant Harbor' in Chinese) is located on the southern coast of China at the point where the Pearl River Estuary joins the South China Sea. It is well known for its expansive skyline, deep natural harbor, and extreme population density (more than seven million inhabitants in an area of less than 426 square miles.

The fact that there was so little flat land available forced the city to build up rather than out, earning it the title of 'World's most vertical city'.

Hong Kong has a highly developed transportation network that is used by more than 90 percent of its population. That network relies on a combination of car, bus, and rail travel, all powered by diesel and the internal combustion engine.

Air pollution is a serious problem.

Sean was made aware of that problem as the Gulfstream began its final approach to Hong Kong International Airport.

"Look at the smog!" He exclaimed as he stared at the city appearing out of the mist just ahead of the plane.

"Los Angeles used to be that way on a bad day," Farrell told him, taking a quick look. "Until the Feds got the car manufacturers to cut emissions." He shrugged. "Of course, LA still has more than enough smog," he smiled and shook his head. "And a bunch of other problems, too!"

"It looks like they built the airport on an island just outside the city!"

"Close," Farrell smiled again. "In this case, they had to build the island before they could build the airport."

"What do you mean?" Sean asked, frowning.

"It sounds weird but it's true." Farrell took another look out the window. "They used fill from inland to create the first part of the island, then, as they dug foundations and laid down runways, they used the waste from those procedures to make the rest of the island--Chek Lap Kok, they call it."

"So they built a whole island out of nothing but that?" Sean shook his head. "Impressive!"

"Wait until you see the city. Some of the buildings are really amazing!"

"How do we get from the island to the city?"

"I assume that there'll be a car waiting for us along with someone from the Company to help us get through customs." Farrell smiled. "I'd hate to have to check my guns at the door!"

As it happened, there was someone waiting for them—a nattily-dressed young Chinese man who greeted them with a smile.

"Mr. Farrell, Mr. Piper." He gave a small bow. "I am Bruce Lee." His smile widened. "Really! My parents, James Lee and Mary Li were huge fans and decided to name me after him."

"Can you fight as well as he did?" Sean asked.

"Alas, no." Bruce Lee shrugged. "But fortunately I do not need such skills—Hong Kong is a modern and very peaceful city." He led them through customs, waving at the agents there as he did so.

They waved back—then turned back to other incoming tourists and businessmen.

"I hope you did not bring too many weapons," he smiled. "Mr. Kelly would be most upset if you started a war with the Chinese."

"We have nothing aside from our personal weapons," Farrell shook his head. "And we have no intention of doing any shooting here."

31

"In that case," he smiled. "All will be well." He gestured them toward the nearby rail station. "The train will be here in a moment."

"Train?" Sean asked.

"Indeed!" Lee nodded. "It is far faster than using a car--we will take the Airport Express. It is a dedicated rail link provided by the Mass Transit Railway and has only three stops," he held up his hand and counted down on his fingers. "At Tsing Yi Island, the West Kowloon Cultural District, and, finally, at Hong Kong Station." He smiled at the two men. "Which is where we will get off."

"When will we see Mr. Kelly?" Farrell asked.

"He is waiting for you at his offices." He smiled. "They are quite near the station." Lee looked into the older agent's face. "Is this satisfactory?"

"It'll be fine." Farrell shook his head. "Just fine."

"Good," Lee nodded as a train pulled in, then gestured his charges forward and helped them board and find seats near the front. "This is a very fast train--it will only take a few minutes to reach our destination." He looked at Farrell. "You bags will be delivered directly to the hotel by a special service." He raised an eyebrow. "I hope that is satisfactory?"

"Fine," Farrell nodded. "And very efficient."

"We try," Lee answered.

So smooth was the train's motion that Sean didn't even realize it had started moving until the landscape began rolling past. After that, he kept his eyes trained out the front windows—and the rapidly

32

enlarging city of Hong Kong emerging out of the smog before them.

"Quite a place," he told the young Asian. "Those buildings look taller than the ones in New York."

"They are," Lee replied. "Hong Kong's skyline is considered one of the best in the world, and you can see how the mountains and Harbor complement the skyscrapers." He made a grand gesture. "Every night, many of the buildings light up in a synchronized show—'A Symphony of Lights' which is, according to the Guinness Book of World Records, the largest permanent light and sound festival in the world.

"Pretty proud of your city, aren't you?" Farrell put in.

"I grew up here." Lee looked out at the city as it grew closer. "It is my home."

"It's beautiful." Sean told him. "And I'll look forward to see that 'Symphony of Light thing."

"I will take you myself," Bruce lee's smile grew wider. "After you complete your mission, of course."

"Of course."

Sean watched as, the train, true to 'Bruce Lee's' promise, completed its quite-short journey and pulled into the central Hong Kong station.

Lee led them out of the station and up the street outside the main doors.

"Where are we going now?"

"We go to that building—just a few blocks from here," Lee pointed to a complexly shaped construct on the opposite side of the road. "Mr.

Kelly's offices are there and he asked me to bring you directly to him."

"That's probably a good idea," Farrell nodded. "The sooner we get started on this mission, the better."

"Mr. Kelly thought you would prefer that." Lee led them through a double door and into a block of elevators. "The office is on the eighteenth floor." He pressed a button and ushered his two guests into an elevator car to the right. "He is waiting there for you to arrive."

The elevator started upward at surprising speed. Its glass front offering a view of the Hong Kong skyline as it moved.

***

Brian Kelly was waiting for them when the door to the CIA suite opened. Sean saw a tall man with a once-athletic build now thickening with fat. Kelly's face was sallow, with pallid cast of someone who seldom ventured out of doors. His hair had once been dark but was now nearly all gray and starting to recede at the temples.

The eyes, however, belied the run-down look of the man's body. They were sharp, intelligent, and observant—and clearly doing their best to avoid looking at Sean.

Instead, they turned to focus on Farrell.

"Frank," Kelly nodded. "Been a long time."

"Yep," Farrell gestured to his side. "I don't think you've met my new partner--Sean Piper."

"Piper?" Kelly's eyes shifted to Sean's face. "Robert's son?"

Sean said nothing.

"I knew your father well, young man." Kelly took a long step forward and extended his hand. "It's a pleasure to meet you."

"Mr. Farrell's told me all about your relationship with my father. " Sean responded coldly ignoring the proffered hand. He held the big CIA man's eyes then smiled mirthlessly and finished with an icy: "Captain."

"Shhh!" Kelly looked around the area in which he'd chosen to meet the two men. The CIA offices in this building were of the 'railroad' type—running in a straight line away from the elevators. The front area held a small couch and a reception desk with doors on either side, each, Sean assumed, leading deeper into the suite.

The desk was manned by an ageless Asian woman who had nodded and smiled at Bruce as they entered.

Girlfriend? Sean wondered as he saw Bruce's answering smile. "No," he decided when he saw that the woman was certainly too old for. Mother maybe, Sean nodded slowly. A relative of some kind for sure...

After greeting the woman, Bruce took a position in front of the door, standing guard while Kelly met his visitors.

"I'd prefer not explaining that nickname to the staff here." Kelly put a hand on Sean's shoulder and guided him to a door beyond the desk, motioning for Farrell to join them. "Besides, it really has no place in this discussion."

He led them through the door into what Sean decided must be his own office. There was a desk at the far end of the room, fronted by a few chairs.

A second desk—smaller—was set at a right angle to the first. A very young and very attractive Asian woman sat there, working at a desktop computer.

"Linda...," Kelly said as he led Sean and Farrell toward the larger desk.

The younger woman—clearly Kelly's private secretary--looked up and smiled in her boss's direction.

"Take the rest of the morning off—I'll be in conference until after lunch."

"Are you sure you won't need me to take notes?"

"No notes." Kelly shook his head. "And if you are asked, I didn't come into the office at all this morning." He raised an eyebrow. "Understand?"

"Yes sir." The girl tapped the papers in front of her into a neat pile, than put them into a drawer which she immediately locked. "I haven't seen you today." She suddenly smiled. "Perhaps I will after lunch?"

"Perhaps." Kelly gestured toward the door. "We'll see." His eyes stayed on the young woman as she crossed the room and left, then: "Lock the door, Bruce," the young agent had followed behind Sean and Farrell. "Let's try to keep this as private as possible."

Lee snapped the door lock into place and took a stance alongside, relaxed but ready for anything.

"Now gentlemen," Kelly dropped into his office chair. "Let's get down to business." His eyes skated over Sean and came to rest on Farrell. "We can talk about old times after we're done."

"All right," Farrell tapped his fingers together. "Tell us what you know about the Chinese hack of the Office of Personnel Management."

"Not much," Kelly leaned back, thinking. "We traced the IP address to a military office near Beijing. That wasn't a surprise—we've seen that IP address—and that office location—several times in the past. It's been the launching site for a number of attacks of this sort over the past few months."

"What do you know about the hackers who work in that office, sir?" Sean asked.

"I know that they're all quite young, the most promising members of various technical schools scattered across the People's Republic. They are trained by the best hackers the Chinese can get their hands on." He raised an eyebrow. "And these days, they're not afraid to practice their skills against American interests."

"The attack on OPM," Farrell spoke up. "You're quite sure that it came from inside Chinese territory?"

"That's what I told Langley—the State Department people came to the same conclusion."

Farrell nodded, then: "Show him, Sean."

The younger agent reached into his bag and pulled out a tablet. "This is an analysis of the OPM hack." He put the device on Kelly's desk. "You can see that it was, indeed, initiated from the IP address you're aware of, but note this secondary address—the one that infiltrated OPM financial records."

"I see what you mean." Kelly stared at the data, tapping a finger on the desk. "Have you traced the location of this second IP?"

"It came from somewhere inside Hong Kong," Sean opened his arms. "From this part of the city."

"You want me to help you find out who was behind this part of the larger hack…"

"Just help us find the target," Farrell told him. "We'll do the rest."

"Who are you working for on this one, Frank?" Kelly stared at his old friend. "I know you have CIA paperwork but this isn't their kind of operation." He frowned. "Just who do you report to these days?"

"I'm part of a special operations team." Farrell didn't bother telling the Hong Kong chief that he and Sean were the team. "We report directly to Mary Max Holston."

"The Mary Max?"

"There's only one."

"You have moved up in the world!" Kelly shook his head. "And I thought I was doing well…"

"Just get us the information we need," Farrell cut in. "And we'll be out of your hair in no time."

Kelly nodded. "I'll get my people on this right away—and in the meantime," he looked at Sean. "Perhaps you'd be my guests for lunch? I'd like the opportunity to tell young Mr. Piper my side of the story."

***

As Kelly led Piper and Farrell out of the massive building complex which held his office (Sean trying hard not to goggle at the architecture around him), a car was threading down a narrow street some three thousand miles to the east…

***

"At least it has cooled off!" Raghib Azimi muttered from the passenger seat of the aging Honda Civic.

"Yes, from one hundred three degrees to a mere ninety seven." The driver, Aabid Lodi, chuckled as he waited for the traffic light to change. "It is Allah's curse on those who have turned their backs upon him!"

"Hot or cold, it matters not to me." Azimi pulled a 9mm pistol from his belt, stroking the long silencer he'd slotted onto its barrel with loving hands. "Not when we do God's work!"

"Put that down!" Lodi scanned the area around them, worried about prying eyes. "We don't want any warnings about our coming to be spread!"

The turned a corner, and increased speed as they gained access to the Shaheed-e-Millat Expressway.

"Where is the office we are looking for?" Lodi asked as he passed an overburdened truck wobbling along one side of the road.

"It is on Siraj-ud-Daula road—we must get off there."

The drive was not a long one and so, a few minutes later, they exited the expressway and drove a short distance down the indicated road, finally pulling into the parking lot of the Askari Degree College.

"Keep the weapon hidden," Lodi told his partner. "And do not use it unless there is no other choice." He stepped out of the car. "We must not allow ourselves to fail in this mission!"

The other man nodded and slid the pistol under his shirt as, side by side, the two walked across the parking lot to the entrance of the College.

"We are here to see Professor Rahman," Aabid Lodi smiled as he spoke to the police guard at the door. "Can you tell us what room he is using?"

"Is he expecting you?" The man looked down at a list on his desk. "I have no indications…"

"Tell us where he is!" Azimi drew his pistol and slammed the barrel against the policeman's forehead. "Now!"

"Fool!" Lodi drew his own weapon. "I told you not to keep that hidden!"

"We cannot be stopped by such as this!" Azimi snarled. "He must tell us what we need to know!"

The policeman, stunned, looked at the two men before him, eyes dully recording the pistols pointed at him.

"Where is Rahman?" Lodi asked again, placing the muzzle of his weapon directly between the guard's eyes. "Where?"

The guard just stared for a moment, then, quite unexpectedly, he acted, pushing the barrel of the pistol away from him with his left hand while pressing a button with his right.

The hallway was suddenly filled with the wail of a siren.

"This is your fault, idiot!" Lodi slammed his own pistol down on the guard's head—hard enough that the stricken man slumped to the floor. "Now how are we to find out target?"

"He was looking at a list…" Azimi grabbed the papers on the guard's desk and began shuffling through them. "It must show…" He slammed a finger down on one of the papers. "Here! Rahman is in room 115." He looked to the side, saw a map of the building and pointed down a nearby hall. "We must go that way!"

The two men left the unconscious guard behind and ran down the hallway, their guns now at the ready.

From time to time, a door would open a crack—then quickly close when the student or teacher inside saw the drawn weapons.

"They will call more police," Lodi yelled above the cacophony of the siren. "We must hurry!"

"There!" Azimi pointed at a door. "That is room 115!"

The two men raced to the door, Azimi getting their first and grabbing the door knob…

"It's locked!" He growled.

"Stand back!" Lodi pointed his pistol at the doorknob and fired, the sound of the silenced shot undetectable in the continuing din of the alarm.

The bullet dug into the wood of the door—and did nothing to the lock.

"You must hit the lock itself!" Azimi yelled— and Lodi tried with four shots in rapid succession.

All to no effect.

He was about to try again when he felt something smash into his side. He lost his balance for a moment, staggered a step forward, and fell against the door.

"I…" He put a hand against his side, felt something wet and sticky. "I've been shot!"

"The Police!" Aziumi turned to look up the hall, ducking as he saw a uniformed man fire in his direction. "What do we do?"

41

"There is only one thing we can do." Lodi pulled his shirt open, revealing the explosive vest beneath. He grabbed the detonating mechanism, wrapped his hand around the cheap plastic handle of lanyard.

"ALLAHU ACKBAR!" He screamed at the top of his lungs—and yanked hard.

The resulting explosion shook the building on its foundation.

But the door to room 115 remained closed and locked.

***

"I did not desert the boy's father!" Brian Kelly's tone was firm. "I was ordered to stand down!" He looked at Sean, spreading his arms. "I obeyed that order—and I still don't know if I did the right thing! I have dreams..."

"You should have had my back!" Farrell's voice was quiet, sure. "You owed me that much."

"Yeah." Kelly nodded. "You might be right about that; I did owe you that much—and a lot more." He looked at the two men sitting across the table from him. "But it's too late to do anything about it now." He sighed. "Way too late."

"I have just one question," Sean had listened to the older men argue all through lunch. He knew that Kelly was telling the truth—he also knew that the man had been unable--or unwilling--to go against orders. "What," he looked into Kelly's eyes. "Would you do if the same thing happened again?"

"I don't know." Kelly shook his head. "Really, I have no idea. I'd like to think I'd do the right thing..." Kelly leaned back in his seat, took a sip of the scotch he had ordered, and looked—really looked—into the younger man's eyes. "I really had no choice …

CHAPTER FOUR

Umar Ah Chong sighed as he entered the restaurant. He was uneasy about attacking an infidel here—in the very heart of the city—but his Imam had been quite insistent.

Just as insistent as he had been the day he tried to talk Umar into changing his family name to 'Awang' because it was "More Muslim."

The Imam is Malay, he told himself. His people have always assumed that they are the only pure Muslims, although it is well known that Chinese Muslims have a stronger faith!

Umar knew that many of those Chinese who converted to Islam were far more pious then Muslim-born Malays who were, he knew, of questionable devotion.

I will prove my devotion today, he told himself. Prove it in a way that cannot be questioned!

He saw his target near the rear wall of the restaurant and headed in that direction, his hand going to the silenced pistol he had thrust into his belt.

***

"…So I held my men back." Kelly looked at Sean, eyes troubled—he wasn't ready to leave the subject yet—not until he had explained himself further. "There weren't enough of them to do any good anyway, and if we had gone to the site in question, we would certainly have been killed."

"So you were afraid," Sean had heard the story three times now—and he was pretty sure he knew exactly why Kelly had done what he had done. "Afraid of dying, afraid of getting in trouble."

Kelly thought for a long second, and then raised his eyebrows in something approaching surprise. "I guess…" He looked at Sean. "I guess I was."

"Okay," Sean nodded. "I can understand that. Dad always said that fear was a great motivator— for good or evil." He looked at Farrell. "I'm willing to let it go if you are."

"I have to think about that," the older man said, eyes hooded. "Maybe…"

There was a commotion behind them as a man pushed his way between two tables crowded near the center of the room, upsetting one diner's cup of tea in the process.

For a split second, his chair back pushed his jacket up, the hem sticking in the gap between table and chair.

"That man has a gun!" Sean noted. "Is that normal in Hong Kong?"

Kelly turned and took a look. "He could be plainclothes police, or…"

The man drew his pistol and pointed it in the direction of their table.

"Down!" Sean shouted, throwing himself to the floor and tipping the table over to give the three men seated around it some cover.

The intruder's pistol fired three times, the silenced barrel muffling the sound.

"Crap!" Kelly pulled out a phone. "I told Lee to stay back in the office!" He looked at his companions. "Are you two carrying?"

"We left our weapons with our luggage," Farrell told him. "We didn't think we'd need

45

them..." He ducked back as three more shots smashed into the thick wood of the table, causing cracks to appear in the sheltering surface.

"We've got to do something!" Sean grabbed a knife that had fallen in his direction when he upended the table.

"I'm all for that," Kelly peeked out from behind the table—and ducked back as two more shots clacked out. "He's getting kind of close."

"Give me the knife," Farrell told his partner.

Sean handed it to him. "What are you going to do?"

"Get ready to move. When I say now..." Farrell suddenly stood up and threw the knife at the gunman. "Now!"

Sean slid out from his side of the table and ran directly at the gunman. He was lucky—the man ducked away from the oncoming blade leaving him completely out of position to do anything about Sean. And he was close enough that, before he could once again raise his pistol, Sean was on him, his hand closing around the shooter's wrist.

Sean twisted outward--hard.

The gun clattered to the floor.

Sean smashed an elbow into the man's face, driving him back and across another table just as the diners seated there scurried away.

The attacker slumped giving Sean took an opportunity to turn and look for the gun.

It had slid under a nearby table—one occupied by three screaming Chinese women.

"Sean!" Farrell yelled. "Behind you!"

Sean whirled just in time to see the attacker fumble for the detonating lanyard on what he could now see was an explosive vest.

Shit! The world suddenly began to move very slowly as it always did when Sean found himself in a fight. He knew he didn't have enough time to reach useful cover. He also knew that if the vest was detonated, many of the diners crowded around them would be hurt, perhaps killed.

There was only one thing he could do.

He abandoned any thought of reaching the gun and leaped at the would-be bomber, grabbing the hand that was already reaching for the lanyard. The man desperately trying to pull free, clawing Sean's face with his left hand while fighting to free his right from the young agent's iron grip.

"Don't kill him!" Farrell called out. "We need to question him!"

Easy for you to say, Sean thought as he slammed an elbow into his opponent's face, breaking the man's nose and spattering himself and those still milling around with blood and snot.

The man staggered for an instant, his free hand going—quite involuntarily—to his savaged nose. That instant of relief allowed Sean to drive his heel into his opponent's kneecap.

Something snapped—and the man, with Sean still holding onto his right hand, crumpled to the ground.

Right next to the knife Farrell had thrown at him.

Sean drove his knee into the moaning man's chest just under the rib cage, driving the breath out of him, rolling away for a moment to grab the knife lying on the floor.

We want him alive, Sean thought as his hand closed around the plastic hilt of the cheap blade. I can't just cut his throat. His left hand was still locked on the others right wrist as he rolled back and drove his forearm into the other man's face, drawing another gasp and a momentary cessation of the man's struggle.

Sean took advantage of that, pushing his opponent's right hand flat against the floor before raising the knife before driving the rather blunt point through the man's palm and deep into the wooden floor beneath.

The man screamed as blood spurted—and tried to reach the lanyard with his left hand.

Sean didn't give him the chance. He drove his elbow into the man's temple with savage strength.

His opponent went limp and Sean hit him again, and again, and again …

Until the man slumped, unconscious, into the steadily growing pool of his own blood.

"Nicely done," Farrell told his partner as, the fight over, Sean's world began to slow down to normal speeds. "Now keep him nice and still while I get the vest off."

Sean did as directed, pushing the man flat against the floor while Farrell unbuckled the suicide vest and yanked it off the man's left shoulder.

"Okay, got it—and the lanyard is well away from him." He looked at his partner. "You can free his hand."

Sean grabbed the hilt of the knife and pulled.

It didn't move.

"You're stronger than you think." Farrell smiled. "Use your foot for leverage."

Sean did as advised, putting his left foot down next to the man's skewered hand while he got a good grip, before, with one concerted effort, he put his back into another attempt—and staggered back two steps as the knife pulled free.

Farrell immediately pulled the vest free of their attacker, rolling it up and pushing it safely beneath his left arm.

"Kelly!" Farrell turned back to the CIA station chief. "Let's get him out of here!"

"Already on it!" The burly man was on the phone, giving rapid instructions in Chinese. "Lee and some of the others will be here in a few minutes," he told his companions as he pocketed his phone. "They'll clean the mess up and make sure the restaurant staff stays quiet about this." He shook his head. "I hope it doesn't cost too much—my budget is a little strained right now."

"Maybe I should have let him blow the vest?" Sean asked, pulling the man's left arm over his shoulder as Farrell did the same with the right, putting the vest over his outside shoulder. "That way it wouldn't have cost us anything." He glared at Kelly. "Of course, we'd all have been dead..."

"Okay," the CIA man made a quick calming gesture. "I know you're right—it's just that I have to deal with all the administrative bull..." He felt Farrell's eyes on him. "Forget it," he sighed and pointed to the door. "Take him this way!"

"Get the gun." Farrell nodded to the table the weapon had rolled beneath. "We really didn't want to leave it for your men to explain."

"Good thought," Kelly knelt down and retrieved the weapon, sticking it in the back of his belt. "This could be embarrassing."

"Come on," Farrell began to move toward the door, Sean pacing him. "Show us how to get back to your office."

"It's this way," Kelly walked past them and parted the few individuals who tried to ask questions. "Hurry—it won't be long before the cops get wind of this."

Farrell nodded and, with Kelly making a path for them, they quickly carried their unconscious prisoner and his deadly vest out of the restaurant and down the street to the building that held the CIA office.

***

"Did you get anything out of him?" Farrell asked some hours later. He and Sean had taken the time to check into their hotel—Sean wearing a pair of Kelly's pants (three sizes too big) because his own were spattered with blood.

While he was showering and changing, Kelly's people transported their captive to a safe house and began interrogation.

"It's too soon for us to have gotten a whole lot," the CIA chief told them. "We know he's a Chinese Muslim—there are a fair number of them scattered around the city—and he says his Imam told him that what he had to do to us."

"Us?" Farrell asked. "Or you."

Kelly's eyes narrowed. "What makes you say that?"

"We're new to Hong Kong—no one here is likely to know anything about us."

"Yeah, but…"

"No buts. You've been the CIA Station chief for some time, right?"

"Almost eight years," Kelly looked at Sean. "After I left the sandbox, I spent time at the Presidio," he shrugged. "I learned to speak a couple of Chinese dialects at the language school there."

"Made you the perfect candidate for this post," the youngster nodded.

"So you've been here eight years and no one has tried to kill you—until now."

"Which would argue he was after you two. After all, you just arrived and I've been here for all this time…"

"Think about the location where he made the attempt—we went to that restaurant because you brought us there—nobody had any way to know who we were…"

"But they had to know who I was." Kelly nodded and tapped the intercom on his desk. "Mary—did I have any visitors today?"

"A man came just after you left for lunch," she told him. "I told him where to find you." There was a brief pause. "Oh!" The girl gasped. "Was that the man with the explosive vest…?"

"Have Bruce show you a photo—I want to know if he's the one that came looking for me."

Another pause—this one a little bit longer as she called the big Asian agent and waited for him to send an image to her cell phone.

She gasped when it arrived. "He's definitely the one, Mr. Kelly. He said he needed to talk to you about an urgent matter. I didn't know…"

51

"It's all right, Mary." Kelly interrupted her. "You had no reason to suspect anything." He looked at the others. "But I would appreciate it if you'd be good enough to tell Bruce to bring the office to Security One and set a guard on the door—we don't want another such visitor, now do we?"

"No sir."

"That's a good girl." Kelly smiled. "Let me know when Bruce finishes his preparations."

"I will, sir."

Kelly released the intercom switch and turned to Farrell. "You're right. He was after me. But why?"

"Something has changed—something that connects you to the other killings we've been dealing with—and the other individuals whose identities became known to their enemies."

"Have either of you had anything to do with an academic named 'Rahman'?" Sean interrupted. He'd just finished booting up his tablet for the first time since exiting the plane and had discovered an alert waiting. "He's Pakistani."

"It couldn't be Hanai Rahman could it?" Farrell asked, turning toward Kelly. "Do you remember him, Kek?"

"Please don't call me that," the burly man said, glancing around the office. "I do remember a Hanai Rahman—but I thought we brought him back to the states and gave him asylum there." The two men turned toward Sean.

"This guy wasn't in the US," the youngster said, looking at the report on his tablet. "He was a Professor at some college just outside Karachi." He bent to look at the screen a bit more closely. "His name was Hanai, though."

"Where's your secure phone," Farrell asked. "I need to check on this."

"Over here," Kelly stood up and gestured to his own seat. "I hope we're wrong and it's not our Hanai Rahman—he was a good guy."

"He's not dead," Sean told them. "A pair of gunmen attempted to kill him—but he barricaded himself inside a classroom and they couldn't get the door open." He scrolled down a bit. "One of the gunmen had a suicide vest and set it off—the blast didn't penetrate the door although it did a job on the two gunmen." He shrugged. "Pakistani intelligence is looking into it but so far they have no leads and no information that's of any use."

"Hanai Rahman was a CIA informant during the war in Afghanistan." Kelly told the young agent while Farrell made his call. "He gave us a lot of good intel about leaks in the Pakistani government," he grinned. "Not to mention telling us all about the ongoing difficulties inside the Pakistan Intelligence Community."

"Community?" Sean frowned. "More than one agency?"

"Pakistan is weird," Kelly told him. "There is no fixed official name for their intelligences services. Instead, they have one supposedly cooperative federation." He shrugged. "We just call the whole mess the "Pakistan Intelligence Community" and leave it at that."

"And this Rahman was a member of that community?"

"Not exactly," Kelly shook his head. "He was a teacher at one of their colleges—an expert in codes and computers—they occasionally consulted with him when they thought someone had broken one of their cyphers or hacked into their mainframe." Kelly smiled. "Once, when the Pakistanis were thinking about selling one of their nukes to an Al Qaeda cell in Yemen, he called us from right inside a government office!"

"And told us everything we needed to know so we could stop the sale," Farrell finished. "He was the one attacked at the school all right—Mary Max says he's okay if a bit shaken."

"Any idea who was behind the attempt?"

"No. But I think it's all instigated from one place—from the people who got into the CIA payment book and are handing out information on the names inside it."

"My name would be in there," Kelly nodded slowly. "From the time I spent in Kuwait during the Gulf War…"

"And that's why they came after you—and will probably come again." Farrell raised an eyebrow. "Unless we stop them." He looked at the Station Chief. "You were going to brief us about hackers in Hong Kong?"

***

Imam Kasim Rageah suspected the worst when Umar Ah Chong failed to return from his assignment and there was no report of an explosion on the news.

He has failed, the Imam told himself. I should have known better than to send a Chinese convert to do the work of Allah. He thought about his congregation, and began to measure them one against the other. Only a true believer can accomplish this task!

A name came to him—the name of a young man he had come to trust and admire for the purity of his devotion to the prophet.

Youssou Alassana! The tall young man in question came from a Sengalese family who had joined the mosque immediately upon their arrival in Hong Kong. Youssou's father worked in the financial sector, his mother, Aminata, busied herself with a woman's work—often cleaning Rageah's own mosque!

The Imam smiled at that thought. Aminata Youssou is a good woman—one who has never tried to do the work of men! Instead she has remained in the home and the Mosque and done those things a good Muslim woman should do.

He thought of her son. Youssou is nearly twenty now, Rageah told himself. He is straight and tall and strong.

He was suddenly certain—so certain that Allah himself must have spoken to him. Youssou can do what must be done! Rageah nodded with satisfaction. He will succeed where the unworthy Umar failed.

Rageah walked to his desk and picked up his cell phone, bringing up the Alassana family's number.

***

"The IP address that I separated from the rest of the Office of Personnel hack indicates that it came from this part of the city." Sean circled an area of Hong Kong that ranged from the tall buildings and

International businesses to the seaside. "I can't break it down further than that."

"You don't have to," Kelly looked at the map. "I happen to know that there's a sort of hacker commune in that area." He pointed toward the shore. "A group of young men and women who make their living doing odd jobs with computers." He shook his head. "I wouldn't have thought they'd be involved in something like this, though."

"We'll need to talk to them," Farrell put in. "Try to find out if it was one of them who stole the data or, if not, who they think might be guilty."

"That might be a problem," Kelly ran a hand down the side of his face. "That's not really the 'nice' part of the city—it's filled with radicals of all kinds." He looked at his two companions. "Not the place to take a quiet stroll."

"What else can we do?" Farrell asked him. "We have to find out!"

"There might be another way." Kelly thought for a long moment, then: activated his intercom. "Mary?" He waited for her reply. "Do we still have the number of that computer consultant?

"The one off Che Kung Miu Road in Tai Wai District?"

"Yes."

"I think so." There was a pause. "Yes, I have it here."

"Give them a call and see if they can come up here sometime tomorrow—the earlier the better."

"Yes sir."

"And Mary…"

"Sir?"

"Tell them to call before they come to the door."

"Yes sir."

Kelly turned to the others. "No use taking chances." He stood up. "Now, are you two ready to have a talk with our guest?"

"Indeed," Farrell answered. "I have a few questions for him."

Sean just nodded, unsure of what would be expected of him in such an interrogation—and equally unsure about how far he would be willing to go to get answers.

Time to find out, he thought, following the others out the door.

CHAPTER FIVE

Youssou Alassana stopped short as he saw his target walk out of the building just across the street from his position.

That is the man! He thought, his hand unconsciously reaching for the pistol he'd secured under his jacket. The man the Imam says must be killed!

He started to draw the weapon but froze when he was jostled by one of the many workers spilling out of buildings all around him.

It is too public here, he watched as his target slid into the back seat of a cab. I might be stopped before I accomplish my mission.

Youssou watched as two more men entered the cab. I must follow, he told himself, signaling for another of the colorful vehicles that trolled the city streets searching for fares. Follow them until they reach their destination…

Another cab pulled up and the tall young Sengalese Muslim climbed in, instructing the driver to follow the other cab that was, as he pointed it out, pulling away from the curb.

Then I will do as I've been ordered, Youssou smiled a secret smile as he stroked the grip of his pistol. And kill the infidel—along with all those in his company!

***

"Have your men learned anything?" Farrell asked as they walked up a concrete path toward a smallish building in the Wah Tat Industrial complex.

"He hasn't said much," Kelly shrugged. "Just that he was ordered to kill the Infidel," he spread his hands. "That's me, by the way—you were right about that."

"Ordered by whom?" Sean asked.

"He won't say." Kelly knocked on the door of the building. "I have people looking into his background, checking out his job, his family…"

"He's Muslim, right?" Sean waited for Kelly to nod. "Do we know what Mosque he frequents?"

"I don't think so," Kelly held up a hand as a tallish Asian opened the door. "Let's find out."

The interior of the building was bare of anything that might be called an amenity. The floor was concrete as were the walls. There were no windows of any size and what light there was came by way of the two bare bulbs hanging down from the ceiling.

A single chair stood near the center of the space, the slumped figure of a man sitting in it.

"Has he said anything more?" Kelly asked the man who had opened the door.

"No sir," the Asian was tall—nearly six feet, and light-skinned—with a battered face and a nose that showed signs of multiple breaks and hard, strong hands—the hands of a laborer—or an interrogator.

"We have tried to reason with him, when that did no good, we told him what will happen to him if he refuses to co-operate …"

"What would that be?" Sean asked, eyes on the man in the chair. "Will you beat the information out of him?"

"If we have to," Kelly answered. "Don't forget that he was perfectly prepared to kill everyone in that restaurant to get me."

"Yeah," Sean nodded. "But we're supposed to be better than that."

"This isn't a job for a 'better' man," Farrell told him. "It's for one who gets the job done—whatever it takes."

"Maybe." Sean walked over to the chair and looked the captive over.

The man in the chair was staring at the floor. His broken nose had been attended to—rather rudely—but at least he could breathe freely. Both the man's eyes were quite black, and his lip was split.

"Did you beat him up?" Sean said, glancing at Kelly's agent.

"He didn't do any of that," Kelly answered. "All he did was snap his nose back into place—you were the one who did all that other damage."

Sean frowned and turned back toward the man in the chair. I knew I was the one who broke his nose, he studied the black eyes. I guess the eyes are on me too, he remembered hitting the man with a forearm and an elbow. And the lip …

He rubbed his chin. Damn, I did all of this! He leaned closer. I wonder if he recognizes me…

The man looked into Sean's face. Fear suddenly appeared in his dark eyes.

Guess he does! Sean hid a smile and spoke to the captive: "You know who I am, don't you."

The man nodded.

"I could have killed you."

Another nod.

"Perhaps I should have killed you."

More nods.

"Tell me what I want to know," Sean reached out and touched the man's ruined nose, smiling as the captive pulled back. "Tell me now!"

The man glared at him, hatred—and fear—stark in his face.

"Tell me now," Sean kept his tone even. "Tell me or I will be forced to take action…"

"Please," the man suddenly pleaded. "Please don't hurt me! I have a wife and a small child…"

"There were many small children in the restaurant," Sean locked eyes with the captive. "You would have killed them without a second thought."

"I had no choice," the man shook his head. "It was the will of Allah!"

"Did Allah speak to you directly?" Sean leaned closer.

"No," the man shook his head again. "He spoke through the Imam. The holy man."

"And that Imam's name is?" Sean held the man's eyes, doing his best to keep a stern look on his face.

"Kasim Rageah," the man closed his eyes as he spoke. "Imam Kasim Rageah told me it was my duty to kill that one," he nodded toward the watching Kelly. "I do not know why."

"Thank you." Sean patted his cheek, smiling as the man tried to pull away. "That is what I needed to know. And now…"

Before he could finish the sentence, the door burst open and a tall black man rushed inside, a pistol in his hand.

Before anyone could react, he opened fire.

CHAPTER SIX

Jason Manners, or, as he had decided to call himself, Dakheel Intsham, looked at the body of his mother.

She was a traitor to the Prophet, he told himself. A whore who gave herself to an Infidel!

Jason had learned a great deal about his parents in the last few days—ever since he had found Imam Waahid.

He told me the truth about my parents, he thought. Even as he showed me the secrets of the true religion!

There were very few Muslims in Montana and Jason, despite his mother's profession of the faith, had been forced to turn to the internet for a teacher to guide his steps into Islam.

For a time, he had followed the teachings of an Imam in Brookings—but he soon grew bored with the man's continuous talk of peace and coexistence.

Jason didn't want to coexist with anyone. His life had not been a happy one. Cursed with poor eyesight and a body that was never as tall or strong as that of his contemporaries, he had turned to the Qua'ran for the fulfillment he couldn't find in his actual life, becoming something of a scholar in the ways of the Prophet.

At sixteen, he had finally found what he was looking for--a view of Islam that empowered him by showing him that, as one of the truly faithful, he was more powerful than those around him.

Self-radicalized, he had gone from website to website until he had found Waahid. The Imam had taken Jason by the hand and shown him everything he needed to know, shown him the way to reach Paradise where he would no longer be small and helpless...

Today, he was putting the Imam's teachings and directions into play.

His father was away—out of town on some kind of business—but his mother, his whore of a mother, was home and within his reach. He had savored the look in her eyes when he had driven the long-bladed knife he had purchased through EBay into her belly—a look that had gone from horror to agony when he twisted the blade before ripping it free.

He watched as her intestines, wet with blood, dropped out onto the floor and listened as she moaned and cried and begged...

Begged him!

He'd savored every moment of her agony, watching her until the very moment that she died.

Now, with the still blood-stained knife scabbarded on one side of his belt and his father's service automatic pistol secured on the other, Dakheel Intsham prepared to carry out the remainder of his mission.

James Riordan was a teacher at the local school—as was his wife, Donna. Waahid had shown then-Jason the proof of the man's past—a past in which he'd flown Drones for the CIA, raining death down on the few men of the faith with the courage to fight against their Infidel oppressors.

Riordan had been responsible for the deaths of several Al Qaeda and Hamas leaders—and now it was time for him to pay.

Once-Jason, now Dakheel, made a last check of his pistol, then, without a backward glance, walked out of his parent's house, his destiny before him. It took him less than ten minutes to walk from his place to the Riordan home. It was a pleasant enough journey—the sun was warm on his back, the flowers were blooming, and the birds were singing in the trees on both sides of the street.

This is what Paradise will be like, he thought. A place filled peace and beauty—along with my seventy-two virgins!

Dakheel/Jason was looking forward to that reward with great anticipation—after all, he was, himself, a virgin.

The Riordan house was on the corner, surrounded by a chain-link fence. Dakheel/Jason went to the front gate and let himself in.

Mr. Riordan might be around back, he told himself. It's nearly dinnertime and I know he likes to barbecue.

With that thought in mind, Dakheel/Jason bypassed the front door and walked along the river rock pathway toward the back of the house.

Riordan had gathered the rocks by himself, then laid out the path and dug it out deep enough to hold them. Jason's mother had admired the look of it and asked his Dad to build something like that for them.

Nothing had come of it.

Dakheel/Jason went around the house and turned toward the wide patio that filled most of the back yard. The Riordans were, as he had expected, on that patio busily preparing dinner.

"Jason?" Mrs. Riordan had been his Tenth Grade English Teacher the year before. "Can we do something for you?"

Dakheel/Jason kept walking, his right hand drifting until it touched the grip of his father's gun.

"Come on over," Mr. Riordan's voice was deep and friendly. "Can we offer you a hamburger? We have plenty…"

Dakheel/Jason walked to within ten feet of the big teacher—and drew his pistol.

"Jason?"

"I am no longer Jason," the youngster intoned. "I am now Dakheel Intsham." He raised the pistol. "And it is time for you to pay for your crimes against Islam!"

Dakheel pulled the trigger.

Nothing happened.

"Jason!" Riordan took a step toward him, eyes troubled. "What's wrong?"

The safety! Dakheel/Jason fumbled with the metal switch. I didn't take the safety off! He finally felt it click into the proper position.

"I told you," he raised the weapon, centering it on the big teacher's chest. "I am Dakheel Intsham." He looked at the other man's face. "And it is time for you to die!"

He pulled the trigger.

This time it fired.

The 9mm bullet took James Riordan in the chest, punching through the right lung.

He staggered back a step, his mouth gaping in surprise and shock.

66

"I don't…"

Dakheel fired again, stepping closer.

Riordan fell to his knees.

Another shot—another…

Blood spurted from James Riordan as he fell; face forward, into the grass of his own backyard.

"James!" Mrs. Riordan rushed to the stricken man's side. "James! For the love of God!"

"Yes," Dakheel nodded. "For the love of God!" He took another step forward and pointed the pistol at Mrs. Riordan's head.

She didn't turn around, just cradled her husband's head in her arms as he fired.

It is done! He told himself as he looked over the crumpled bodies.

Sirens sounded in the distance—coming closer by the second.

Now it is time for me to claim my seventy-two virgins. He turned toward the front of the house, his pistol held loosely in his hand as he waited for the police to arrive…

***

"Allahu Ackbar!" The attacker screamed as he fired at the knot of men in the center of the room. "Death to Infidels!"

Sean dropped down behind the chair—and the now-frightened man sitting in it. He drew the pistol he'd strapped on after visiting his hotel and clicked the safety off…

He was targeting the attacker when a flurry of gunfire came from the other end of the room.

***

"He's dead," Farrell stood up from the body near the front door.

67

"This one too," Sean noted—the man in the chair had taken several bullets all of which had, without question, been meant for Sean. "Any idea who he is?"

"Not a clue," Kelly shook his head. "It would have been nice to take him alive."

"We had no opportunity to do that," the tall, distinguished-looking Asian who had shot the man shook his head once, his large caliber handgun smoking in his hand—still too hot to re-holster. "One of you would certainly have been killed had I not acted when I did."

"He's right," Sean said. "I was aiming to kill too."

"And me," Farrell added. "It would have been too dangerous to do anything else."

"So we're at a dead end?" Kelly asked.

"I don't think so," Sean nodded toward the dead man in the chair. "Our friend from the Restaurant told me that he was ordered to kill you by his Imam."

"There are any number of Imam's in this city!" Kelly told him.

"How many named 'Kasim Rageah'?"

"James?" Kelly looked at his agent. "Ring any bells?"

"No," the Asian shrugged. "But it should be easy enough to find a Mosque run by a man of that name." He pulled a cell phone out of his pocket. "I'll get Mary working on it right away."

"So what do we do with the bodies?"

"I will take care of them," the Asian agent smiled. "Do not worry—they will not be found."

"I don't think I introduced you," Kelly put a hand on the tall Asian's shoulder. "This is James Lee." He smiled. "Or rather, Senior Inspector Lee of the Hong Kong Police."

"Gentlemen," Lee gave a slight bow.

"You're a cop?" Sean said, eyes wide with surprise.

"I am in charge of the local region." Lee nodded. "Which includes this industrial complex."

"But…"

"My job is to keep the peace," the Inspector fixed Sean with a jaundiced eye. "No matter what actions that goal might require of me."

"And we really appreciate the help," Farrell said, putting a hand on Sean's arm before the younger man could say more. "I'm sure Mr. Kelly will keep you informed as to our progress."

"I will indeed," Kelly slapped the other man on the shoulder. "Shall I give your wife our best when we return to the office?"

"Of course," Lee smiled. "And tell her that I said you must join us for dinner someday soon."

"As soon as this business is over," Kelly matched the other man's smile. "I promise."

"Good." Lee raised an eyebrow. "Please do not let these Muslims kill you. Mary would lose a very good job—and she would never forgive me for allowing that to happen."

"I give you my word that I will do my very best to stay alive." Kelly solemnly returned as he executed a sketchy bow of his own. "And I will be in contact very soon—after we investigate this Imam."

"I will wait to hear from you." Lee gestured toward the door. "Now go—and let me handle this mess."

"Thank you," Kelly told him.

"Indeed," Farrell added a small bow of his own. "Many thanks."

Sean copied his partner—then quickly stepped into the open air. He's a cop, he told himself. A high-ranking cop whose wife works for Kelly! He looked back at the small building and thought about what was inside. We left him with two dead men—and he's not the least bit concerned about getting rid of their bodies!

Sean shook his head. This is not the world I grew up in!

He stepped to the curb as Kelly signaled a cab to pick them up...

***

Sean's tablet was where he had left it—on the corner of Kelly's desk—he'd left it there to keep it safe while they checked out the prisoner.

It bleeped a signal as soon as he turned it back on. "There's more trouble back home!" He told his partner as he waited for it to show him the report it had decided was part of his investigation.

"What is it this time?" Farrell had been hoping that nothing further had happened yet. "Another killing?"

"More than one," Sean studied the information on the tablet's screen. "A teenaged Muslim in Montana killed his mother with a knife, than shot a couple of neighbors before getting into a gunfight with the local police." He shook his head.

"Everyone involved is dead—including two of the cops."

"There are Muslims in Montana?"

"Not a lot of them," Sean queried the tablet. "About point 34 percent of the population." He shook his head. "There're only about a million people in Montana so if we do the math," he put numbers into a program, looked at the answer. "There are only about thirty four thousand Muslims in the whole state."

"And one of them caused all this?"

"Looks like," Sean stared at the screen. "Not much more information than that. I wonder why my program…"

Farrell's cell phone began to ring.

"I think we're about to find out," the older man pressed the 'ANSWER' button. "Hi Mary Max, what's up?"

Sean watched his face change as their superior spoke.

"Yes, I understand." He nodded at whatever was said. "Forty eight hours." He nodded again. "Yes Ma'am, I'll report to you then." His mouth curled up as if he'd bitten into something sour. "Yes, I promise." He listened a moment longer, then punched the 'OFF' button and looked at Sean. "One of the teachers in Montana was named Riordan." He sighed. "He used to work for me."

"CIA?"

"Yeah," Farrell nodded. "Drone pilot—good one, too. Mary Max is getting kind of concerned. She wants us to find something soon otherwise Justice is going to get involved."

"What can the Justice Department do that we can't?"

"They can muddy the damn waters—pull any reference to 'Islamic extremists' out of the story. Make it all quietly disappear."

"We can't let that happen! Too many people are involved."

"I agree," Farrell stood up. "Let's see if our friends here have found your Imam-- maybe we can find out just how he found out who Kelly is and why he wants to kill him."

"Don't forget the hackers." Sean nodded slowly. "They were going to try to bring in one of the leaders of the local Hacker community."

"One or the other—we need a lead to follow." Farrell motioned for Sean to follow him. "Come on; let's see how much they've found out."

As it turned out, they had found nothing whatsoever—yet. They had heard from the 'computer consultants' who had promised to send a representative the next day.

That promise allowed Farrell and Sean—who had been on the go for nearly forty-eight hours—to return to the hotel and get some rest.

Both slept badly.

***

"Good morning, gentlemen," Kelly greeted them as they entered his office the next morning. "This is Victoria Liú," he smiled. "Our friend from the 'Computer Consultants Group'.

Sean found himself staring at the newcomer—with good reason. Victoria Liu was a very striking woman. She was tall--nearly as tall as Farrell who stood five feet ten, and slender, with long legs and a classically beautiful face.

"Close your mouth," Farrell whispered into Sean's ear. "You're about to start drooling!" He yanked his young partner's arm and pulled him down to a seat alongside his before turning his attention back toward the woman. "Ms. Liu," Farrell began, giving her a slight bow. "I'm told you know a great deal about computers and their use here in Hong Kong."

The girl smiled—which brought a low-pitched sigh from Sean. "My friends and I are hackers, Mr. Farrell." The smile widened. "As I'm sure you know."

"And right now we need the help of a skilled hacker," Farrell continued. "Has Mr. Kelly told you about our problem?"

"Mr. Kelly has told me nothing. He has been waiting for you to arrive." Liu's hands came out, palms up. "Perhaps you can tell me what it is you want to know?"

"Someone recently hacked into a very important US government data base." Farrell's eyes met the girl's. "Whoever did it is giving the names they found there to some very bad people..."

"Does this have something to do with the various murders that have occurred in your United States over the past few days?"

"We think so."

"I read a statement from your government that indicated the large-scale hack on your government was perpetrated by the Chinese." She raised an eyebrow. "Was that statement in error?"

"The Chinese did hack our Office of Personnel Management," Sean said, leaning forward. "But another entity—as yet unknown to us—used the breach to access another data set—a financial data set."

"And you know this how?"

"I examined the computer records of the hacks—and back-tracked two IP addresses. One came from inside Mainland China, the second—the one that breached the more sensitive data set—came from this island."

"You are sure?"

"I am."

"Interesting." Ms. Liu tapped a perfectly manicured fingernail on her front teeth. "I assure you it was not done by my people."

Sean nodded, eyes locked on that fingernail.

"So," she smiled as she saw where the young man was looking. "What would you like me and my friends to do about this problem of yours?"

"I need help to track down the location of the IP address in question." Sean's eyes met hers, his determination evident. "I don't have the resources to do that on my own and Mr. Kelly here," he nodded to the Station Chief. "Cannot give me what I want."

"But you think I can?"

"If you and your people are as skilled as Mr. Kelly says…" Sean shrugged. "I think it would be child's play."

"I see." She tapped her front tooth again. "Then you are offering us a contract?"

"Yes." Kelly nodded. "Until this is settled."

"I will have to consult with my friends," the girl bit on her lower lip. "If this second hack was a government operation…"

"It would be dangerous for you to look into it." Kelly nodded again. "We understand that."

"Give me two hours," she looked around the office, eyes searching those of the three men watching her. "I will have a final answer for you then."

"Two hours is acceptable," Kelly told her. "Shall we meet here?"

"That will be fine." She stood up and turned toward the door. "I hope we can work with you," she stopped for a moment, eyes turning toward Sean. "It might be…" She smiled. "Interesting."

Then she was gone, a slight breath of her perfume that only evidence that she had been there at all.

"That is a very together young woman." Farrell declared.

"She has to be," Kelly told him. "If she and her 'friends' got caught hacking into Government files, they'd be declared traitors and executed."

"That would be a waste," Farrell shook his head, eyes on Sean. "Wouldn't it?"

"Yeah," Sean nodded. "A waste…"

Farrell laughed and slapped the young man on the shoulder. "Come on, Sean, wake up! This is serious business and if you allow a pretty girl to turn your head…"

"Someone will lop it off," Kelly finished.

"I guess." Sean sighed. "She was awfully pretty, though."

"That she was—and now we have to wait two hours for her to come back unless," Farrell turned to Kelly. "You found some information on Imam Kasim Rageah."

"As it happens," the station chief smiled. "My people did locate a mosque run by someone names Kasim Rageah. It's in the New Territories—near the West Gate."

"How far from here?"

"By cab—anywhere from ten minutes to two hours," Kelly shrugged. "Depending on the traffic."

"Train?"

"Faster—but there might be trouble with your weapons—some stations have metal detectors."

"So what can we do?"

"We," Kelly stood. "Can have breakfast until Ms. Liu returned—once we have finished with her, we can travel to the New Territories and investigate this mysterious Imam."

"Don't you ever think of anything except your stomach?" Farrell shook his head.

"I think of many things," Kelly grinned and patted his somewhat expansive belly. "But these days, I tend to worry about eating first."

"All right," Farrell shook his head. "Let's eat." He looked at the station chief. "I don't suppose there's any place around here to get some ham and eggs?"

"Not to mention omelets and the best hash browns you've ever tasted!" Kelly grinned. "And it's less than half a block from here."

He rose to his feet and headed for the door. "Coming?" He asked over his shoulder.

***

'Pop's' served a breakfast every bit as good as Kelly had suggested. The cook—'Pop'--came out to meet them afterwards. He was a rather overweight Asian who had gone to the University of Virginia to study commerce, working at a local Waffle House to pay the bills.

When he graduated and returned to Hong Kong, he'd discovered that there was far more money to be made cooking eggs than there was working at a commodities desk and so he'd started the thriving business that they now found themselves enjoying.

"Mr. Kelly was right," Farrell told him. "These hash browns are the best I've ever had."

"The trick is to use the very best potatoes you can find," 'Pop' told him smiling. "And cook them in the grease and fat left over from yesterday's breakfast."

They all laughed and Farrell promised that they would return for another meal before they left Hong Kong.

They were just finishing up when Bruce Lee arrived.

"Mr. Kelly," his eyes roamed the room, looking for danger, as he spoke to his boss. "Ms. Liu has returned."

"Good," Kelly stood up. "Take care of the check and meet us in the office." He gestured for Sean and Farrell to join him. "The sooner we get her started on her end of this job, the better."

"What if she says no?" Sean asked as they headed for the door.

"She won't," Kelly's voice showed complete confidence. "Unless the Chinese government is

77

behind the second hack." He smiled. "Which means her refusal would tell us something all by itself."

"I hope you're right." Sean told him. "I'm not sure how we would proceed if we can't find a way to track that IP address."

"Can't you get a physical address from Washington?" Kelly asked.

"I could if they had the right data in their system," he shook his head. "But they don't."

"Then let's hope that Ms. Liu is ready to give us what we want,"

"The computer information would be sufficient for me—Sean, however, might want just a little bit more from the young lady." Farrell grinned as he watched his partner blush at the implication.

"Don't screw around with Ms. Liu," Kelly told them. "She has a lot of friends in this city—and a lot of secrets in her head. Pissing her off could lead to real trouble."

"We have no intention of screwing around with Ms. Liu." Farrell turned to his partner. "Do we, Sean?" He asked innocently

"No sir." The younger agent shook his head, his own tone innocence itself. "No intention at all."

"You're getting better at the lying thing," Farrell chuckled. "Keep practicing."

Sean glared at his partner as Kelly let out a bray of a laugh...

***

He still lives! Kasim Rageah had travelled into the western part of the city to check on his prey—and found him laughing and joking with two other men. Youssou Alassana has failed me! He must have grown frightened and run away. He looked around, fear suddenly dulling his mind. Perhaps he went so far as to tell the police what I ordered him to do. Perhaps even now they are breaking into my Mosque...

Kasim pushed the fear away and closed his eyes for a moment while he regained his mental balance.

No. He shook his head. Youssou Alessiani would not do such a thing. If he failed to kill this man... he watched as Kelly crossed the street and stepped into a tall office building there. It can only be because he failed while attempting to act! He considered that--and realized that he would have heard from Youssou's mother had her son ended up in police custody.

Youssou must be dead! Certainty of that fact filled Kasim. Those men killed him! He nodded slowly. They must have killed Umar Ah Chong as well. A small smile crossed his lips—he had not been mistaken in sending the Chinese Muslim, the man had been true—just not up to the task before him.

I must find someone who will not fail, he told himself as he turned away from the city center. Someone who will not—cannot--be deterred! An avenger who will accomplish the task before the infidels have an opportunity to defend themselves. He smiled as he realized that he knew the perfect individual for the job.

Satisfied with his morning's work, Kasim Rageah headed for the train station. He had work that must be completed before it was time for the day's cycle of prayers to begin.

79

***

In Melbourne, Australia the Namaze Janaza—the prayer for forgiveness of the dead—had begun.

The mosque was nearly full with every adult Muslim male in the community in attendance.

All were involved with the Takbirs when the ceremony was interrupted.

"Dalal Houssani!" A large, heavily bearded man stepped into the prayer hall, eyes darting across those inside. "Which of you is Dalal Houssani!"

Eyes turned to the far side of the room where several women were praying together.

"Dalal Houssani! " The man turned in the same direction. "Show yourself!"

There was a stir among the women and one of them stepped forward.

"I am Dalal Houssani," a middle-aged woman with black hair and tired eyes stated. "Who interrupts this service to call me?"

"I am Adi!" The man snarled, stepping forward.

"I know no Adil." The woman said.

"Not Adil," the bearded man snapped. "Adi—Justice!" He pulled a long-bladed knife from inside his jacket. "I have come to attain justice for those you wronged in Afghanistan."

"Wait!" The Imam stepped into the bearded man's path. "What do you think you are doing? This is a place of God! We are…"

The bearded man swung his long knife in a looping backhand blow—one that nearly separated the Imam's head from his body.

Blood spurted as the holy man's dead body dropped to the tiled floor.

80

"Let no one else attempt to stop me," the bearded man snapped the blade to his side, cleaning it of blood. "I am here to do the holy work of Allah!"

He prowled forward, walking between men who cowered from him until he finally found himself face-to-face with the woman who called herself Dalal Houssani.

"It is known that you accompanied the infidel army into Afghanistan," the man told her. "It is known that you helped them kill many of the faithful.

"I killed as many of the Taliban as I could," she all but spat into his face. "I only wished that I had been able to reach more of the scum."

"That will never happen," the bearded man pulled his blade back and swung with every iota of strength in his body.

Men and women alike screamed as Dalal's head fell free, bouncing once on the tiled floor before rolling to a stop a few feet away, eyes open and staring accusingly at the men of the mosque who backed away, terrified, while her attacker calmly walked out of the building.

CHAPTER SEVEN

"Have your people found any information on this Kasim Rageah person?" Farrell asked as they returned to Kelly's office.

"Not much," the station chief nodded at his aide. "Bruce?"

"Kasim Rageah came to Hong Kong three years ago," the tall Asian glanced at a notepad he'd taken from his pocket. "He established a mosque in the territories almost immediately." He looked at Farrell and Sean. "There are many Chinese Muslims—so many that the Hui were even allowed to protest against the state during the Cultural Revolution." He turned a page, "Kasim Rageah's mosque, however, caters to Muslims who were born outside the People's Republic—mainly Africans and Indonesians."

"The man who tried to kill us yesterday," Farrell leaned forward. "He was clearly African."

"Probably Sengalese," Bruce told him. "There is a colony of such people near the mosque in question—I am sure that most if not all of them count Kasim Rageah as their Imam."

"Bruce," Sean looked at the tall Asian. "Can you get a schematic of the Mosque? It might help us get what we are really looking for."

"I already have one," the aide smiled, holding up a printed map. "I assumed that you might want such a thing."

"Good." Sean looked at his companions. "What are we waiting for? Let's go pay the good Imam a visit."

"Exactly what we had in mind." Kelly nodded and motioned to his aide. "But this time, we'll bring a little extra firepower along."

A moment later, Farrell, Sean, Kelly, Bruce, and three other men were in a silvery van and heading for the territories and the Mosque of Kasim Rageah.

***

"There's been another killing," Sean reported as the van inched through heavy traffic. "In Australia this time."

"Not one of ours, then."

"I'm not sure." Sean skimmed the information. "The target was a woman named 'Dalal Houssami.'"

"Delilah?" Farrell turned to look at his partner. "They got Delilah?"

"Bulletin says her name was 'Dalal'."

"Same name," Farrell shook his head. "Different dialect." He pursed his lips. "She was a very special woman—not afraid to stand up to those around her. I thought…"

"She was on your payroll?" Kelly put in.

"For a time," Farrell nodded. "She worked in our Embassy in Baghdad, and then moved to Syria." He looked at the others. "There she acted as a go-between for the Free Syrian Army." He sighed. "When that 'line in the sand' our President drew turned out to be nothing more than rhetoric, we pulled her out and set her up with an identity in Australia." He looked at Sean. "Too many people that trusted us are gone—we've got to find out who's behind this and keep them from killing anyone else."

"We may find what we need in this Kasim fellow's mosque—and I have an idea how we might accomplish that."

He leaned closer, mapping out his plan to the others.

"Sounds good to me," Kelly smiled.

"Me too," Farrell glanced at his companion. "As long as they don't kill Captain Kelly while we're inside."

"Who is Captain Kelly?" Bruce asked without taking his eyes off the slowly moving traffic.

"We'll tell you later," Farrell told him. "For now," he glared at the traffic. "Just get us to the New Territories!"

***

'Hong Kong Island was ceded to Britain in 1842', Sean had decided to learn what he could about their destination and so, as their van crawled along, he consulted the internet for some background. 'Those parts of Kowloon south of Boundary Street and Stonecutters Island were added to the lease in 1860.'

He scanned down.

'After the Chinese were defeated in the First Sino-Japanese War Britain began to fear for the security of Hong Kong so, using the most favored nation clause that it had negotiated with Peking, the United Kingdom demanded the extension of Kowloon so it could act as a buffer against the growing influence of the French in southern China. The extension of Kowloon was called the New

Territories and added 365 square miles to the British lease—increasing the size of the original colony of Hong Kong twelve times over!'

The van went over a bridge and Sean lost Wi-Fi.

"Is it true that the New Territories are twelve times as big as Hong Kong?" He asked Kelly as he waited for the Wi-Fi to return.

"Maybe a little more than that," the CIA chief answered. "Lots of businesses have moved to the territories to spread out and gain more horizontal space." He shook his head. "The banks and big international companies lease most of the office space on the island—that makes it hard for newcomers to acquire real estate."

"What's your company called?" Farrell asked. "The one that's the cover for your operation." He raised an eyebrow. "I figure you had to move away from the Embassy when the British turned the island over to the Chinese government."

"You'll laugh," Kelly told him. "If you check the directory on our building, you'll find that we are 'Universal Exports'."

"You're kidding!"

"Nope." The burly man shook his head, smiling. "I was kind of surprised that nobody in CIA gave me a hard time when I sent them the paperwork. I guess they just didn't get it."

"Get what?" Sean asked. "What's unusual about calling your company 'Universal Exports?"

"Ever read Ian Fleming's 'James Bond' books?"

"I've seen the movies…"

"Not the same thing." Kelly shook his head. "Although in some of the early Sean Connery films…"

"What our esteemed CIA chief is trying to tell you," Farrell cut in. "Is that 'Universal Exports' was the cover name for various fronts of the British Secret Service in the world of Fleming's James Bond."

"Isn't that kind of advertising who you are?"

"Everyone knows who I am," Kelly told him. "Just as they know that the 'Cultural Attaché' in the average embassy is CIA." He shrugged. "It just seemed a bit more entertaining this way."

"We are almost there," Bruce suddenly cut in. "Just another half mile or so."

"Go around the block a couple of times," Kelly instructed him. "We'll have a good look at the place before we make our move."

"Yes sir," Bruce nodded. "If our GPS is correct, the mosque is on the next block." He nodded toward the windshield. "On the left."

"Okay," Kelly motioned. "Slow down…"

They all stared at the building in question. It was completely unremarkable, looking just like the houses on either side.

"Not very distinctive," Farrell noted. "Let's see what the back looks like."

The back was as unassuming as the front— although both Sean and Farrell noted the existence of a rear entrance.

"What now?"

"Go around again," Sean said. "This time, slow down as you get to the back." He touched the rear door latch. "I'll get out as you do."

"Get out?"

"Yeah," Sean nodded. "While you guys go in the front door and make a fuss, I'm going to sneak in the back and look for the good Imam's computer." He grinned. "If I can find it, it might save us all a lot of trouble."

They passed the front of the 'mosque' again. This time they saw a handful of people entering.

"It's almost time for Dhuhr, Kelly noted. "The mid-day prayer."

"Might be a good thing," Farrell put in. "More people might keep things from getting out of hand."

"Or we might be really badly outnumbered!" Kelly responded.

"Either way." The van made the first turn. "Get ready Sean."

The youngster nodded, checked that his weapon was snug in its holster and the portable hard drive he'd brought was secure in his pocket.

"Coming up on the back of the Mosque!"

Sean took a firm grip on the latch and opened the door...

Before stepping out of the slow-moving vehicle.

***

That wasn't too difficult, Sean thought as he staggered a few feet before regaining his balance. Now let's hope it was worth it!

He ran to the back of the building that he knew held his target and looked around.

No guards outside, he stepped to the back door he'd seen from the car and checked the knob. Locked. He moved to a window and peered under an ill-fitting curtain into the room beyond. Jackpot!

The room was clearly the Imam's personal office, with a large desk pushed against the wall that lay under the window.

And a desktop computer standing on the corner of that desk.

Now to find a way to get inside…

Sean looked at the lock on the back door. It was simple enough—and he'd gotten a few lessons on how pick locks during his short stay at the CIA instructional facility—the 'Farm'—but he hadn't yet quite mastered the art—and this wasn't the time to get more practice.

Gotta get in and out as quickly as I can, he thought as he took out his pocketknife and opened the long blade. If I can slide the blade over the end of the bolt… The lock was old, as was the door. Sun and weather had loosened things enough that…

The blade slid into place and, with a steady push, Sean was able to push the bolt back into the door.

He held it there and gently pushed the door open.

Okay, he looked around. I'm in and there's nobody here. He could hear a quiet murmur from further inside the building. The congregation is busy with the mid-day prayer. He nodded. That should tie the Imam up long enough for me to do what I came here to do.

He moved to the computer and powered the machine up. I don't have time to go through everything on this guy's hard-drive, so…

He placed the portable memory he'd brought onto the edge of the desk and attached it to the

Imam's computer. It'll be safer to just copy everything and...

There was a sudden rumble of sound behind him.

Farrell and Kelly just came in, he realized as the copy program started. I hope they can keep everyone occupied long enough for me to finish this.

Seconds passed. The copy was thirty percent finished. Forty. Sixty. Eighty...

The back door opened and a voice called out in a language Sean didn't recognize. He looked up.

At the biggest, blackest woman he'd ever seen.

She must work for the Imam, he thought, glancing at the copy which had just hit eighty-five percent. He took a closer look at her face as she took a step toward him. She looks kind of familiar, I wonder...

She began to yell at him, her voice rising as he gave her no reply.

Ninety-five percent. Sean held up his hand, trying to slow her down as...

The computer gave a soft ping as the copy was completed.

Sean quickly unplugged the portable memory and stored it in a pocket before he turned to the enormous woman and smiled. "I'll just be going now," he told her, enunciating very carefully. "If you'll just step out of the way..."

She screamed something at him and charged, slamming into his midsection and driving him backwards—into the door that led to the public room...

***

Farrell had no idea what they were going to say to the Imam and his flock—all he wanted to do was stir things up a little bit and cause a little chaos to buy the time that Sean needed to look at the man's computer.

The mosque was a bit shabbier than he expected—he'd seen many during his time in Iraq and Afghanistan as well as a few in the United States—but this one was quite different from all of them.

"I thought Mosques were supposed to be clean," he whispered to Kelly. "This place is filthy!"

"The Imam may be having a problem with his flock," the CIA Chief noted. "From the few remarks I'm hearing, he's not exactly worshipped by most of the men here."

"He's really glaring at you," Farrell observed. "He definitely knows who you are."

"Yeah," the other man nodded. "I guess we know who's been trying to kill me."

"Let's make sure he doesn't try again right now!" Farrell took a step forward and the Imam turned in his direction. "Let's see what he has to say for himself." He took a few steps between the prayer rugs of the kneeling Muslims, his eyes fixed on the man at the head of the group. "Are you Kasim Rageah?" He called out in English.

"The entire room looked at him questioningly."

"Kelly!" Farrell turned to his companion. "Translate!"

The burly man nodded and repeated Farrell's question in Mandarin."

90

The congregants turned toward their Imam, wondering what this was about. Before they could find out, the door that led to the back of the building suddenly exploded open and Sean fell into the prayer hall, the giant woman on top of him.

"Sean!" Farrell moved in the younger agent's direction, gesturing for Kelly to hold his position.

He needn't have bothered. Sean had no interest in fighting with the woman—but he wasn't going to let her pin him to the floor in the middle of what might be a mob of enemies. Instead he slapped his palms against her ears—hard enough to stun her but not, he hoped, with enough force to permanently damage her hearing.

It worked—the woman gave out a sharp cry and grabbed her ears, giving Sean room to roll away.

"Get out of here, Farrell!" He yelled as he banged into the back wall and got to his feet. "Get out now!"

Kasim stood frozen, unable to process what was going on in front of him. He had seen Sean before—on the street with the CIA man and his companions. He was an infidel in my office, he finally realized. If he got into my computer...

He raised a hand and pointed at Sean. "Stop him!" He screamed. "Stop the infidel!"

A man in front of Sean tried—he came upright, still on his knees (he'd been praying to Mecca) and made a grab for the young man.

Sean didn't even slow down. He straight-armed his would-be captor and kept right on going.

"Get out of here!" He waved to Farrell and the others. "Now!"

Then more men started to rise, most of them between Sean and his partner.

"Crap," Sean muttered while he began the task of fighting his way through the crowd. He still didn't know whose side these men were on and he didn't want to start a war with the Chinese, so...

Hands only, he told himself. And nothing fatal!

With that tenet in mind, he backhanded the first man to reach for him, then grabbed the arm of the second and spun him into the third, all the time moving toward the door.

Nearby, Farrell had also gone into action—he fought his way to the door a bit more roughly than Sean, than planted himself in the middle of the portal, holding it open for his partner.

Kelly and Bruce, he noticed, were nowhere to be seen.

"Kill them!" The Imam began to shout. "They must not get away!"

Most of the worshippers looked at him dumbly—they weren't armed and had no intention of killing these men for doing nothing more than visiting the mosque. They wondered if their Imam knew what he was doing—several had been wondering that for some time...

They began to back away, anxious to get out of the fray.

Sean was more than halfway across the floor of the room by now, with only two men in front of him. He sighed when one drew a knife.

I was hoping it wouldn't come to this; he thought as he slid into a fighting posture and threw a feint at the knife-wielder. Come on, he slid forward on the balls of his feet. Don't make this harder than it has to be...

The knife slid down, thrusting toward Sean's midsection—as he had expected. He sidestepped the attack and grabbed the man's wrist with both his hands, twisting his arm to the right and upwards.

The man moaned and dropped the blade.

"Hurry, Sean!" Two of the worshippers had made an attempt to close the door, forcing Farrell to take them down. They lay on the floor at his feet, bleeding from the nose and mouth. "Hurry!"

Sean slammed an elbow into the back of the man's hyperextended arm, dislocating the elbow.

The would-be knife wielder screamed and folded down onto the floor as Sean rushed by him. He was within a few feet of freedom when the first gunshot sounded from behind him—and Farrell groaned as he took a hit.

"Bastards!" Sean whirled, his own gun clearing its holster as he moved. He searched for the gunman—and discovered that the weapon was held in the hands of that enormous woman.

She sighted down on him.

Crap, he thought again, and fired a round into the floor right in front of her feet. She hopped backwards, her own shot going wild.

"Come on, Frank!" Sean grabbed the other man and half-carried, half-threw him out of the door. "Get down!"

He fired two more shots into the room, not really trying to hit anyone, just making sure they kept their heads down. When no more shots came in return, he slammed the door behind him. "Are you badly hurt?"

"I don't think so," the older agent told him. "Come on, we've got to get out of here!"

"Where's the van?" Sean looked toward the street.

"It should be right there," Farrell pointed to a spot across the street. "If Kelly hasn't buggered out…"

"Come on," Sean pulled the other man's arm across his shoulder. "Lean on me!"

The two moved down the walkway to the street beyond. The van was where Farrell said it should be but, as the two men reached the curb, it began to move forward.

"Stop!" Sean held up his free hand. "We're right here!"

For a moment, he thought the van was going to speed by and leave them there but, at the last moment, it skidded to a halt a few feet from them.

"Get inside," Sean pulled the back door open and helped Farrell climb in before throwing himself inside.

"What happened, Kelly?" Farrell snarled. "Couldn't get away fast enough?"

"One of us had to get to the car," the burly CIA chief told him. "We had to get it moving before anyone from the mosque could reach it."

"Yeah," Farrell shook his head. "Sure."

"What happened in there?" Sean asked. "I thought you and Bruce were going to be my back-up?"

"We couldn't get involved in a shoot-out," Kelly said. "The Police…"

"Bruce couldn't help make a path for me?" Sean was frowning now. "He couldn't even do that?"

"Bruce isn't very good at unarmed combat," the other man answered. "Despite the name."

"I see." Sean nodded slowly, eyes hard. "And I suppose you have a bad back?"

Kelly said nothing.

"We've got to get Frank to a hospital." Sean turned to his partner, bending to examine the other man's wound. "He got hit by a stray bullet."

"It's not bad," Farrell told him. "It went through and through and I don't think it hit anything important."

"Are you sure you're okay?" Sean looked into Farrell's eyes.

"We have some people we work with," Kelly told them. "I'll make sure they're waiting for us when we get to the office."

***

"Get them!" Kasim was practically jumping up and down in his excitement. "Don't let them get away!"

"What have they done?" An older man asked him. "Why are you so anxious to hurt them?"

"They are infidels! The worse kinds of unbelievers! The heavy one—he killed our people..." He looked around him, suddenly realizing that all those in the building were Asians. "I mean, he killed our fellow believers..."

"Do you think he came here to harm us?" The older man looked around, frowning. "Did they show any signs of attack before you began yelling?"

"One of them was in my office!" He turned to the imposing form of Aminata Alassana. "You found him there! What was he doing?"

"I cannot say for certain…" The Sengalese woman shook her head. "He was looking at your computer. I thought," she looked at Kasim. "My Youssou disappeared while doing a chore for you." Her eyes bored into his. "Did these men have anything to do with that chore?"

Kasim realized that he had an opportunity here—one that he could use.

"Yes!" He nodded quickly. "I sent Yousou to find the burly man you saw just now." He put a hand on her broad shoulder. "I fear that they did something bad to him."

"Where will they go?" Aminata idly pulled a splinter out of her shin—one of several Sean's shot had sent into her skin. "Where can I find them?"

Kasim quickly told her…

***

"That'll be fine," Farrell nodded, then: "Did you get what we needed?"

"I got everything on his computer," Sean tapped the storage unit in his pocket. "Now I've got to go through it and see what's there."

"You can do that while they're stitching me up," Farrell told him. "No use wasting any time."

CHAPTER EIGHT

Farjad Zarrin sighed as he watched the television news.

It seems that the Americans are about to make a very bad deal with Iran, he thought. A deal that will quickly lead to nuclear war in the Middle East. He shook his head and changed the channel to one showing a vapid game show. It appears that I have done what I have done for nothing...

Farjad Zarrin had been one of Iran's chief scientists, specializing in nuclear research. He had pushed hard for the development of reactors capable of giving the people of Iran all the power they wanted without the unwelcome by-products created by oil and other fossil fuels.

When the regime had approved the research he wanted, he had quickly built the breeder reactors needed to properly enrich the uranium they would need.

But when he started to draw up plans for the next step—the construction of reactors and turbines to create power, he'd been shunted aside and demoted while his team—and it's new, more radical leader--was tasked with further enriching the uranium—enriching it until it could be used for something far more destructive than clean energy.

For a time, Farjad hadn't believed that his government would actually go through with their plans. He'd been happy when the United Nations had finally stepped in and performed inspections of the nuclear sites.

I was sure the regime would come to their senses and use what we had for peaceful purposes...

But they did not. Instead, they intensified their program, even when the other nations put sanctions on the country—sanctions that hurt the very people Farjad had given up so much to help.

It was too much. Farjad could no longer stay in a country that acted with such disregard for its own people. When the opportunity came for him to attend an international convention in Switzerland (with an appropriate guard and 'translator') he had done the only thing his conscience would allow and defected.

It had not been easy. Only the help of an Iranian journalist allowed him to slip away from his watchers and make contact with an agent of the American CIA. That agent had gotten him out of the country and across the ocean to the United States where he had been given the chance to speak out against those who were taking his homeland down the path of war—a war that would kill so many...

And now the Americans have made this terrible deal! He shook his head. They have made me a fool. A laughing stock! He stood up and began to pace the room. What can I do? Who can I talk to?

He stopped his pacing as he heard an odd sound outside his little house.

Odd. He moved to the window. The CIA had put him in what they called a 'Safe House' located at the edge of a military base. When he had spoken out against his country, they had put a twenty-four hour guard on that house, with armed men patrolling front and back to keep him safe.

Now one of those men—the guard at the front of the house—was nowhere to be seen.

Something is wrong! Farjad scanned the yard, searching for any sign of the missing man.

He saw a shadow behind one of the bushes.

Something is very wrong! He turned away from the window and moved toward the kitchen. The phone was there—the special phone that connected him to the guard unit assigned to his protection.

He reached for the phone, his hand brushing against its smooth plastic …

Just as the door opened.

"Farjad Zarrin!" The man in the door was dressed quite simply, with dark pants and a white, short-sleeved shirt.

A shirt that showed a barely-visible red spattering.

"You have betrayed your country," the man produced a large caliber pistol with a long silencer. "You have betrayed Islam!" He lifted the weapon. "For this, you must die!"

Farjad nodded once, almost in agreement.

Then the pistol spat flame and Farjad felt something punch into his chest, knocking him back against the brand new stainless-steel refrigerator his American friends had given him.

He slid down the smooth surface, coughing and fighting for breath. He had not quite reached the floor when the world went dark around him…

***

Sean ignored the signal that told him somebody else on the CIA's 'hidden' payroll had been killed.

99

He was too busy going through the memory from Imam Rageah's computer.

This guy is a real piece of work, he thought. Most of his activity on the internet just involved porn; it's only when you look at his excursions into the 'Darknet' that things get interesting."

Sean had discovered the hidden portions of the internet some years back when he came across a paper titled: 'The Darknet and the Future of Content Distribution' written by a couple of Microsoft employees. It had given him enough information to access a few file sharing sites. His mother had been shocked when he put 'FROZEN' up on the TV months before it was scheduled for release.

After she realized what he had done, she had, of course, punished Sean and forbidden him from doing such a thing again.

He'd more or less obeyed—although he had pulled in a couple of films for his own entertainment (he really hadn't been able to afford first-run films at the time).

Now, using the Imam's browser history and the access program he recovered from the Imam's computer (as well as some programs he'd gotten from the FBI), he took a close look at some very unusual sites.

He had to wade through a number of ISIS and JIHADI sites—most of them featuring videos of beheadings and other 'punishments' to find what he wanted but, finally, he reached a site that was filled with some very interesting information.

"Sean?" Farrell had spent an hour or so being tended to by Kelly's medical friends. As he had surmised, the bullet had been a through and through with no real damage done. The Doctor had cleaned the wound and stitched it shut before shooting Farrell full of antibiotics and telling him to drink a lot of liquid and get some rest.

Rest was out of the question but Sean had persuaded the older man to get some food while he went through the computer files. That had been nearly... Sean looked at the time. Three hours ago! He shook his head. *I didn't realize...*

"What have you found, Sean?"

"A lot," Sean leaned back, rubbing at an ache in his back he'd just discovered he had. "The good Imam has spent a lot of time on various Jihadi sites," he smiled. "Quite a few porn outlets too."

"Did you find anything that would help us?"

"Yeah," Sean turned his computer monitor so his partner could see what was on it. "This is a pay site—you have to pay a fee to get access." He looked at his partner. "The Imam paid the fee and, after browsing through what was available, paid a bigger fee for a list of men and women who are getting money from the US military or one of its intelligence services."

"How is it broken down?"

"By country, I think." Sean put his cursor on the top of one of the columns, clicked on it. "The Imam only paid for Hong Kong, Yemen, and Iraq." He ran down a list of names, stopping when he came to one he recognized. "Here's Brian Kelly," he glanced at his partner. "I guess that's what started all this."

"Is there an address—what do you call it—an IP we can follow up on?"

"Not here," Sean shook his head. "The Darknet is designed to be anonymous—you have to have special software in order to access anything." He gestured toward the screen. "I'm using the same program Rageah has been using or I wouldn't even be able to get this much."

"We still need to track down the other IP address you found, then."

"Yep," Sean turned to his partner. "There's one thing about this that bothers me."

"What's that?"

Sean licked dry lips and brought up the home page of the site he'd been looking through. "Everything here tells me that this is hosted by a server here in Hong Kong."

"We already knew that."

"It's a pay-as-you-go site, I told you that."

Farrell nodded.

"Who do we know that belongs to a 'commune' of hackers here in Hong Kong?"

"Ms. Liu?"

Sean nodded. "Ms. Liu." He sighed. "I have a lot of questions for her when she finally comes back."

***

Aminata Alassana got off the train at Hong Kong station—quite near the address given her by Imam Kasim. She was fairly familiar with the area, having spent a few years working as a maid at one of the downtown hotels that catered to foreign visitors.

I must find 'Universal Exports' she told herself. I know it is in one of those buildings. She looked at the High rises a few blocks away. Once I find the proper office, I will wait until it is deserted, then I will prepare.

She tapped the handgun that weighted down her handbag.

Prepare for the moment when the foreign devils return and I can get my revenge!

She crossed the street, ignoring the horns that blared out, and turned toward the buildings in question.

'Universal Exports' was not, as it happened, very hard to find. It occupied a suite of offices in AIA Central, located in the central part of the city close to the Bank of China Tower.

The site had once been the home of the Furama Kempinski Hotel, which had been famous for its revolving restaurant but until being demolished to make way for the AIG tower which, in 2009, became AIA Central.

Aminata smiled as she looked at the sign proclaiming that 'Universal Exports' was on the 18th Floor, then turned toward the restaurants that she knew were just a block or two away.

She had a few hours before the building emptied out—she might as well have something to eat.

***

"Have we heard from Ms. Liu?" Farrell asked as Kelly came into the office Sean had been using to study the hard drive.

"There was a message," the burly CIA man replied. "She said she'll be in early tomorrow morning—around ten o'clock."

"Any hint on whether her 'commune' is going to work on this for us?"

103

"Nothing—just the time she'll arrive." He looked at Sean. "Did you find anything?"

"Everything," the young agent told him. "Whoever is behind this definitely has the CIA's pay sheet for overseas operatives and in-country assets." He pulled up a page. "This is the Hong Kong section."

Kelly leaned in and looked, shaking his head when he saw his name right at the top of the list of agents in country. "Any hint of who put this out?"

"Nope," Sean told him. "And I can't get much more than the Hong Kong stuff and some names from the Mid-East—the whole thing is set up to work—on a pay per view basis--through a very anonymous portion of the darknet—it may be invitation only but I'm not sure of that."

"How did you get this?"

"Our friend the Imam had already set up...." Sean thought for a moment, then: "I guess you'd call it 'an account'. He has access to names from China, Hong Kong, Afghanistan, and Iraq."

"That's enough!"

"Sure is," Farrell noted. "But I'm worried about the lists that name our agents in Russia, Iran, and Syria."

"The Imam wasn't interested in them," Sean put in. "That's why he doesn't have those names."

"I'll give Langley a call," Kelly told them. "Let them know how serious this really is."

"I'll want to call Mary Max, too." Farrell told him.

"Sure," Kelly gestured to the door. "Use my phone."

"Don't you want to go first?"

"Nope," Kelly looked at his watch. "It's nearly five PM here—that means it's five in the morning back home." He raised an eyebrow. "I really don't want to wake up my boss just yet."

"Crap," Farrell said. "Mary Max will kill me if I wake her up again."

"Why don't we go and have some dinner?" Sean asked. "By the time we're done, it'll be late enough to call Washington without worrying about waking anybody up."

"Good idea." Kelly smiled. "There's a nice little Thai place just a block or so from here."

"Lead on," Sean stood and stretched. "I could eat a horse!"

"Is the data safe?" Farrell asked, glancing at the computer Sean had been using.

"I have it password protected," he shrugged. "It's safe enough unless someone takes the whole PC and if that happens," he tapped his pocket. "I have a copy with me and a second copy on the cloud."

"Sounds good," Kelly nodded. "I'll tell Bruce to stay until we get back—he can keep an eye on things."

"Good enough," Farrell stood up, wincing a little as the stitches in his side pulled. "Let's go."

A moment later they were in the elevator and heading for the street below.

***

Aminata Alassana was just finishing her Kang Keaw Wan when she heard the voices.

Those men are speaking English! She turned in her chair, looking toward the front door of the restaurant. It could not be…

105

But it was! As Aminata watched, open mouthed, the man she was hunting walked through the restaurant's entrance, chatting with two other English-speakers, one of whom she immediately recognized as the young man who had fought with her in the mosque!

Allah has provided! She thought, opening her bag and taking the pistol hidden there out. Praise be to Allah!

She clicked the safety 'OFF', and turned toward the three foreigners, slowing raising the weapon and laying the sights on her primary target—the burly CIA chief.

She squeezed the trigger.

***

"This place is pretty good," Kelly announced as they came through the front door. "The food is very authentic," he looked at Sean. "I hope you like spicy food."

"Love it," the young agent looked around the restaurant floor. "Anything but octopus, I hate..." A flash of burnished metal caught his eye and he found himself staring at a too-familiar mountain of flesh.

"Get down!" He yelled, knocking Kelly to one side and pushing Farrell back.

A shot rang out, the bullet passing between the three men and hitting the door, cracking the glass.

"Who's shooting?" Farrell crouched down behind the maître d's stand and drew his own weapon. I can't see where the shot came from!"

"She was at ten O'clock," Sean had his handgun out and had taken cover behind the bar. "I can't see her now."

It was hard to see anything through the screeching, milling mass of patrons fighting to get out of the restaurant.

"Her?"

"Big black woman—the same one that I had trouble with at the Mosque earlier."

"I don't see anyone like that…" Farrell pushed a couple past him, urging them through the door. "Keep looking!"

Another shot rang out, this one hitting a young woman who was trying to get out from behind a table a few steps in front of Sean.

She screamed in fear and pain.

"We've got to get her soon!" The young agent yelled back. "Before too many innocent bystanders get hit!" He looked around. "Where's Kelly?"

"I don't know," Farrell shook his head. "Probably hiding behind the biggest mob of people he can find!"

"I can't believe…" Something caught Sean's eye. "Two O'clock!"

Farrell swiveled in that direction, caught a glimpse of the woman in question smashing through a door on the side wall. "That was her," he moved forward, motioning the still-milling crowd to go past him and out the door. "She must have gone into the kitchen!"

"Maybe that's where Kelly went!" Sean hurried down one side of the dining room, eyes searching for the target. "I don't see him in here!"

"We're going to have to go in after her and try to save the bastard," Farrell shook his head and pushed a stunned waiter out of the way. "You up for it?"

107

"Better than waiting for her to turn up again," the youngster helped an older woman get up—it was clear that she had hurt a leg and he half-lifted her into a chair, motioning for her to stay there. "Besides, I'd rather take the fight away from this room--there are already a number of wounded."

"Okay," Farrell reached the edge of the kitchen door. "On my mark!"

Sean joined him, hugging the wall opposite his partner. "I go first," he looked into the older man's eyes. "You've already been wounded."

"Go fast, stay low." Farrell shook his head. "And don't hesitate—if you get a target, shoot!"

"You don't have to tell me twice." Sean nodded. "Let's do this!"

"Okay," Farrell smiled. "One," he raised his gun, checked the safety. "Two…"

Before saying another word, Frank Farrell pushed the door open and sped into the kitchen, leaving his partner behind.

"Crap!" Sean swore and slid through the door, moving to the right as he did so. I can't believe he did that!

Sean swept the kitchen, searching for the target—or Kelly. Or, come to that, my partner!

A rustle to his left told him where Farrell was—the older agent had gone to cover behind a large preparation table and was peering over the top. "Get down!" He waved to Sean. "Grab some cover!"

Sean did as he was told, rolling under a metal table to the right of the doorway. Once under shelter, he raised his head up far enough to take a look around the kitchen. It was larger than he

108

would have expected, with several cooking ranges and ovens in sight.

I'll bet they cook for more than one restaurant in here, he told himself. It would be more cost-effective that way…

A movement to the left caught his eye.

It's Kelly! The CIA chief was behind a serving cart of some kind, eyes fixed on something beyond his position. He looks scared! Sean followed his eyeline—and finally saw what the other man was staring at.

There she is! Sean saw the big African woman now—she was just a few feet from Kelly's position, slowly moving toward him behind something big and metallic. He can't hit her, Sean realized. And she can't hit him. He watched the metal cube slide across the floor, getting closer to the CIA chief every second. Yet!

Sean raised his own pistol—and found that he didn't have a clear shot at the woman either—the metal shield covered just enough of her body to make any shot problematic.

I've got to do something; he looked at Farrell who was also trying to get a bead. And quickly.

There was only one thing he could think of that might work.

"Farrell" He called out—and saw the woman suddenly look in his direction. "I'm going to try something."

"Don't' do it, kid!" His partner snarled. "You'll get yourself killed right along with that bastard Kelly."

"Gotta try," Sean smiled. "Cover me, okay?"

"Don't screw up!" Farrell replied, his weapon ready. "I don't want to have to explain this to your Mom."

"No sweat," Sean gathered himself. "On three: One…Two…"

Sean sprinted forward—right at his target. Time slowed—as it always did when he took action—and it seemed to take forever for the woman to even notice him. When she finally did, she slowly turned toward him, her finger tightening on the trigger of her pistol …

It never went off. Before she could fire he had gotten close enough to dive to the floor and slide past her metallic shield.

He fired three times before she even realized she was no longer safe.

***

"Dinner in Hong Kong is certainly exciting," Sean said as he and Farrell exited the restaurant having spent nearly an hour being interviewed by the local police. "And I'm still hungry!"

"You know what they say about Chinese food," his partner smiled.

"Yeah," Sean shook his head. "But I never thought it was true!"

"It's a good thing Kelly has good relations with the local authorities," they turned a corner and headed for the office. "I would hate to have to explain all that to someone not disposed to believe us."

"I'm glad he's good for something," Sean muttered. "He's sure not much use in a fight."

"He used to be," Farrell's mouth tightened. "He used to be one of the best soldiers in the world."

"What happened?"

"I don't know." Farrell shook his head. "I wish I did."

"Are you going to call Mary Max?" Sean opened the door that led into AIA Central. "It's late enough."

"Yeah," Farrell nodded. "She's got to know what's going on."

"Maybe we can order some take-out?" Sean stepped into an elevator car. "I am sort of hungry."

"We'll see if Bruce knows a good place," Farrell smiled. "One that doesn't include a gunfight with each meal!"

They entered the offices of Universal Export, nodded to Bruce, and motioned for him to follow them to Kelly's office.

***

Bruce did know a good restaurant nearby—and offered to personally pick up the food while Farrell and Sean made contact with their boss.

That contact took less time than Farrell had anticipated. Mary Max was pleased that they had found the site which held the CIA paymaster files—and displeased that they hadn't yet found out who had managed to procure them.

"Send me all the information you have via secure e-mail," she told them. "I'll put the FBI onto the Deepweb site—maybe we can find something there."

Sean snorted.

"Yeah," Mary Max snickered. "I agree—that means it's up to you two to find the source of all these deaths." She paused. "There were two more killings today…"

"Nearly three," Farrell told her. "They made two tries at Kelly."

"That wouldn't be much of a loss," she responded. "But we can't let this keep going on— you two need to find the source and plug it— permanently."

She hung up before they could say a thing.

"So," the CIA chief's voice rang out from the doorway behind them. "You talked to Mary Max?"

"She asked me to thank you for handling the cops and local officialdom," Farrell said, turning to look at the burly agent. "It wouldn't do any good to have us locked up, now would it?"

Kelly looked at him for a long moment, then: "What did she really say?"

"Just what I told you." Farrell held the other man's eyes for a long moment. "What did you expect her to say?"

"Nothing." He turned on his heel. "Nothing at all."

CHAPTER NINE

Kasim Rageah waited until after midnight for Aminata Alassana to return to the Mosque. When she did not do so, he checked news sources for any mention of her.

A report of a 'disturbance' at a restaurant caught his eye.

The police aren't saying much about this, he realized, reading through the article. All they will say is that a fight broke out and that shots were fired...

Kasim had a friend who worked for one of the news services, he started to call him then, realizing that it was nearly one A.M., decided to wait until morning.

He went to bed a very worried man. If Aminata had failed, he did not know who to turn to in order to get his mission completed.

Perhaps one of the more recent converts could be talked into doing the job. Many of them—particularly the younger ones—had no love for westerners. If he could convince them that it would be in their best interest to kill the CIA station chief...

He began to think of incentives. Was there anyone prepared for martyrdom?

An idea struck him. What if he didn't try to kill the devil Kelly directly? What if he went at him through those around him?

That might work—and it wouldn't require anyone to expose themselves. He might even be handle it on his own.

A plan started to take form in his mind…

***

Farrell headed for bed after talking to Mary Max, instructing Sean to do the same. The younger man nodded, than ignored the instruction and spent two more hours searching the Imam's browser history.

Aside from his forays into the dark net and his seeming intoxication with porn, nothing else of interest was apparent.

Finally willing to call it a day, Sean yawned and locked up the office computer, unplugged his portable storage unit, tucked it into a pocket, and headed for his hotel.

It was time to get some sleep.

He had planned to shower first, but the bed was too inviting so, mere moments after entering his room, Sean Piper was sprawled atop the covers, fast asleep.

He woke early the next morning and, remembering the two meals he had missed, decided to get some breakfast—after taking a shower.

A half hour later he was back in 'Pop's', the restaurant Kelly had taken he and Farrell to the day before. There he enjoyed peace, quiet, and a 'Waffle House' style omelet complete with more of those great home fries.

Sated, he returned to the hotel to find Farrell still asleep.

Sean left him there, reasoning that it would speed the healing of his friend's wound, and headed for Kelly's office on his own. It was almost nine-thirty and Ms. Liu was due at ten.

The streets were packed with men hurrying to their offices so Sean, who had seen the same type of thing in New York, relaxed and let them sweep him along until he reached the AIA building. At that point he detached himself from the crowd and took the elevator to 'Universal Exports'.

The office was quiet.

"Where is everyone?" Sean asked as he tapped on Kelly's door.

"What do you mean?" The Station Chief stood and looked around. "I don't see…"

He stopped, his eyes on the front door and the desk that faced it.

"That's odd," he stepped out of the office. "Mary is never late! I wonder where she is?"

"Maybe her husband knows?"

"Yeah," Kelly nodded. "Good idea." He pulled out his cell. "I'll give him a call."

Inspector James Lee was at his desk when the call came in—and was surprised by Kelly's question. Mary had left for work as she always did, he told the CIA chief. He couldn't understand why she wasn't already there.

"Have there been any problems with the trains?" Kelly asked him.

"No reports of anything," Lee told him. "You're sure she didn't just go out for coffee or something?"

"She's not here, James." Kelly kept his voice level. "She hasn't been here as far as I can see."

"Go Se!" He replied. "Do you think something has happened to her?"

"I don't know," Kelly shook his head. "I'll start checking on this end."

"As will I from here," Lee's voice was determined. "You will contact me if you learn anything?"

"I will," the CIA chief nodded. "And you will keep in touch with me?"

"Of course."

"Don't worry, my friend." Kelly bit his lower lip and stared at the empty desk. "We will find her."

"I know we will." Lee answered. "Goodbye."

The phone went dead.

"Do you think she got hurt in the street?" Sean asked. "There were a lot of people milling around out there when I came over from the hotel."

"I doubt it." Kelly rubbed at his chin. "She's been coming to this office for nearly five years, I can't believe that she'd have trouble on this day and not on the others."

"What do we do?"

"For now," Kelly shrugged. "We wait and hope…"

The office phone rang.

"Nín hǎo," Kelly answered. "Hello."

"I have Mrs. Lee," a voice intoned in Chinese. "If you want to see her alive, you will come— alone—to Sha Tin station. You will receive more instructions there."

There was a click and the line went dead.

"That voice was familiar," Sean said. "I've heard it recently."

"It was that Imam," Kelly shook his head. "Kasim Rageah."

"What are you going to do?"

"I am going to take the train to Sha Tin Station," Kelly told him. "There's nothing else I can do."

"You're not going alone!"

"I have no choice." He looked at Sean. "Look at you—you'd stand out like a sore thumb!"

"There must be another way."

"None that I can see." Kelly patted him on the back. "Get Farrell, tell him what's happening. I'll contact you if I possibly can."

Sean nodded and watched as Kelly hurried through the door, then he turned to Bruce who had just entered.

"Bruce, I think we need that van of yours again…"

***

Farrell had been slow to wake up when the phone in his room rang—and was surprised at the time when he finally did open his eyes. Those pain pills I took were stronger than I thought, he told himself. I'd better lay off them until the mission is over.

He turned his attention to the phone, lifting the receiver and managing a "Hello".

He came awake when he realized what Sean was telling him.

"So let me see if I have this straight," he said several moments later. "Mary Lee didn't make it to work this morning. Later, Kelly got a call indicating she'd been taken by someone who he assumes is Imam Kasim."

He paused while Sean assured him he had it right.

"He's following the orders he got on that call and heading for a train station in the territories." Farrell nodded. "He wouldn't let you go with him." He nodded again. "Which was a good move—two white men would have been way too easy to spot and track."

Another reply from Sean.

"So he went alone and you grabbed Bruce and are on the way to Kasim's Mosque—you figure Mary's in there somewhere."

And she probably is, Farrell told himself. I doubt the Imam has many more followers who want to go out on missions for him considering what happened to the last few.

"Okay," he sucked at his lower lip as he reached for the transport guide he'd picked up in the lobby. "I'll meet you at…"

Farrell paused at Sean's answer.

"You don't want me to join you?" Farrell raised an eyebrow at that. "You want me to take over the station in case Ms. Liu shows up?" Farrell thought about that for a long moment.

The kid's right, he finally told himself. We have to think of our primary mission here—and we have to talk to Ms. Liu—especially in light of what we found in Imam Kasim's computer…

"Okay," Farrell rubbed the sleep out of his eyes. "You're right—it would be better if I stayed in the office where I can look for Ms. Liu and co-ordinate any other action that might be needed." He threw his feet off the bed and sat up. "Call as soon as you have any information at all." He waited for a second. "And I do mean anything."

He stood up as Sean signed off. A cold shower is called for, he told himself as he headed for the bathroom. I've got to have a clear head when I get into Kelly's office—just in case this all goes to shit...

119

CHAPTER TEN

It took nearly an hour to get to Sha Tin station. The train wasn't all that crowded and the few individuals who were aboard were either headed to the racetrack or the University—and as classes had started several hours earlier, there were very few students aboard.

When they finally pulled into Sha Tin, Kelly got off and stopped, letting the horse players move around him as he took a long look around.

Aside from those forced to detour around him, there was no one paying him the slightest bit of attention.

It wasn't until the station finally cleared that his phone went off.

"I can see that you made it to the Sha Tin," the voice on the other end proclaimed. "I can also see that you're alone." There was a long pause. "Now I want you to get back on the train and go to Tai Po Market—you will get further instructions there."

The phone clicked off.

Kelly sighed and turned back to the tracks—the train he had travelled on to get here was gone— enroute to its next stop.

He found a bench and sat down. It would be ten or twelve long minutes before the next train pulled in.

***

That was far too easy! Kasim Rageah, sitting in the safety of his Mosque told himself, smiling. I knew that his American upbringing would force him to do what I told him—all of these Americans have the firm belief that they are heroes willing to give all to save the damsel in distress.

He laughed, thinking of what he had done with his captive.

I will keep the fool travelling from station to station until after mid-day prayers, then I will direct him to a quiet spot where I can eliminate him—and move on to the next name on my list.

The Imam smiled, pleased with himself.

And once that pig is dead, he told himself. I will take action against the next one. And the next. And the next.

He took his handgun out of a drawer and ran a finger down its smooth barrel.

When I have done all that, I will leave this place and travel to Syria. He smiled. Where I will be welcomed by my brothers of the Islamic State!

There, he thought with a rush of excitement. I will witness the birth of the new Caliphate. A Caliphate that will soon dominate the world!

***

Traffic was, as seemed the norm in Hong Kong, very heavy. Heavy enough that it took Sean and Bruce nearly ninety minutes to make the drive to Kasim Rageah's Mosque in the Territories.

"Just drive on by," Sean told his companion. "And pull around to the back." He glanced at his watch. "Mid-day prayers will begin in about fifteen minutes. I'll try to get in and take a look then."

"I will stay with the van," Bruce told him. "Keep it running in case you need to move quickly."

"That's fine," Sean hadn't expected much help from the big Asian. "I will call your cell if I need you."

The other man nodded and turned onto the street that, they knew, held the Mosque. A half dozen men were in front of the place, talking and smoking as they waited for prayers to begin.

"I hope they stay out here," Sean muttered. "It'll make things easier." He nodded for Bruce to drive on by and go around the corner. As they did so, Sean's phone rang.

"Piper," he answered, eyes on a handful of men walking up the block toward the rear of the mosque.

"Sean," Farrell's voice sounded tight. "Listen, you should know that Ms. Liu has not shown up and I can't reach her cell phone."

"That's not good," Sean motioned for Bruce to slow down. "I hope we haven't scared her away."

"I don't know," Farrell responded. "I'm going to see if there's a way to locate her cell phone. If it's turned on, we might be able to find her."

"Good idea," Sean signaled Bruce to stop and popped the door open. "See what you can do—I'll call back when I finish here."

"Where are you?"

Sean smiled. "I'm on the street at the rear of Kasim's mosque." He hurried toward the door he knew led to the Imam's office. "Hoping that nobody notices that I'm not moving in the same direction as everyone else."

"Be careful," Farrell's voice was sharp. "You know you can't depend on Bruce for much in the way of back-up."

"I know." Sean reached the back wall of the mosque and crouched at the edge of the single window there. "Gotta go," he whispered. "I'll report in after I'm out of here."

Sean clicked the phone off and turned off the ringer, then rose just enough to look through the window.

Kasim was there, bending over a desk drawer. Sean watched as the Imam closed the drawer and turned toward the interior of the mosque.

Mid-day prayer should be starting in a few moments, he told himself. When Kasim goes into the prayer room, I'll make my move.

A few seconds later, the Imam rose and went through the unrepaired door that Sean knew led into the main portion of the mosque. The youngster waited for a count of thirty to make sure the man hadn't forgotten anything, then picked the already damaged door lock (no one had bothered to fix it since Sean's last visit) and slipped into the Imam's office.

He stood there for a moment, listening to the soft murmur of prayer in the room beyond the interior door.

Now, he asked himself. Where should I look for information about Mrs. Lee? Sean stepped to the desk, opening the door that the Imam had been closing a moment ago.

There was a gun inside—a large caliber automatic.

Interesting tool for a man of God or Allah or whatever. Sean picked the gun up, ejected the magazine and worked the slide, catching the single round that had been in the chamber. Keeps it

123

loaded and ready, too. He smiled. But I'm not a thief! He put the now-empty pistol back into the drawer and dumped the magazine and stray bullet into the garbage pail under the Imam's desk.

Now, he looked around. That big woman came at me from over there. Sean headed to one side where he could see a curtain blocking off another doorway. Let's see...

He pushed the curtain aside and froze, shocked. There was a small room behind the curtain, just big enough for a bed and a small table.

He could see a huddled body on the bed, covered with a blanket.

He slipped into the room and gently tugged on the edge of the blanket, revealing what was underneath: the lifeless body of Mrs. Lee.

Crap! Sean leaned in close, trying to find any sign of life. Her face was badly bruised and there was a thin line of blood running from her mouth to the stained mattress beneath.

She wasn't breathing.

She's been badly beaten! He pulled the blanket back, eyes narrowing as he saw that her clothing was torn and disheveled. It looks as if she might also have been molested.

He suddenly realized that Kelly was in grave danger.

I've got to warn him that he's walking into a trap! He pulled out his cell. Gotta let Frank know what's going on—Bruce too!

He didn't know how much time he had before someone came back into the office, so instead of making a call or sending a text, he took a quick picture of Mrs. Lee's brutalized face and sent it out

124

to Farrell, Kelly, and Bruce with a simple note: 'Inside Kasim's Mosque'.

He hit 'SEND' and tenderly covered the body. When he was sure she was properly covered, he turned and made for the door leading into the prayer room.

Sean Piper was angry—angrier than he had been at any other time in his life.

The door hadn't been repaired since his last visit—it was just leaning across the frame. Sean didn't bother to pull it open—he didn't want to waste the time. Instead, he kicked it forward and followed it as it crashed into the room beyond.

CHAPTER ELEVEN

Kasim Rageah spun in alarm as the door behind him splintered and fell onto the prayer room's floor.

"What?" He sputtered—and saw the young American step through the now-open portal.

"You are a monster!" The young man said in English. "You killed that woman in cold blood!"

Kasim turned away from the angry young man and looked into the confused faces of his flock. "This man is an infidel! He must be destroyed! He must be killed!" He turned and pointed at Sean. "Kill him now! Show him the strength of Allah!"

The young man looked at the half-dozen men in the room with disdain. "You follow this creature?" He pointed at Kasim. "A thing that molested a helpless woman and killed her for no good reason?" He took another step. "Is that Allah's will?"

The Asian's stared at him. One or two had a few words of English—they had understood the gist of what he'd said and were turning their gaze toward the Imam.

Those who did not understand stood, unsure of what they should do.

"KILL HIM!" Kasim screamed "DON'T LET HIM GET AWAY!"

One or two of the younger men turned toward Sean, one even took a tentative step in his direction...

Then everyone froze in shock as a massive shock tore through the building as a silvery object crashed through the front door.

She's dead! Kelly stared at the photo on his cellphone for a long second. That damned Imam killed her!

The CIA station chief was still at Sha Tin Station—waiting for the train that would take him to the next location specified by the kidnapper.

I won't be going there now, he told himself as he stood and headed for the stairs. I have a debt to pay elsewhere...

He emerged onto the street and hailed the first Taxi he saw.

Sean held his ground as the silver van pushed its way into the prayer room. The front of the van was smashed flat by the force of the crash—but Bruce was unharmed—as he proved when he emerged from the wrecked vehicle.

"Where is he?" He yelled to Sean, eyes roaming the startled faces around him. "Where's the man who murdered my mother?"

Sean saw the Imam stiffen when he heard the words—and quietly pointed the man out to the tall Asian.

Kasim deserves whatever he gets, Sean told himself. And it's only fair that I give Mary's son the first shot at him.

Bruce seemed to agree. He strode right at the frozen figure of the Imam and lashed out as soon as he was close enough.

The blow knocked Kasim five feet to the side and down to the floor of the Mosque.

Well, Sean thought as he watched the awkward blow. This Bruce Lee really doesn't know how to

127

fight... A smile worked its way across his face. But he's big and strong and has long arms which give him lots of leverage.

He watched as Bruce hauled Kasim upright before hitting him again, knocking him back to the floor.

And he is really pissed off!

Sean heard a mutter from the crowd, saw one of the men produce a knife from somewhere under his clothes.

"No," Sean drew his pistol and shook his head. "Let them work this out one on one."

He knew some of the worshippers had at least a smattering of English—enough that, coupled with the sight of the handgun, kept them frozen in place.

He turned just as Bruce slammed his fist into the Imam's midsection. He should have put that a little lower, Sean thought, critiquing the big Asian's technique in his head. It would have knocked all the breath out of that bastard. Instead...

Kasim ducked the big man's next blow and made to run away—but he couldn't get clear of Bruce's reach in time and was dragged backwards and into another long, looping blow.

Should I stop this? Sean asked himself. Should I do nothing more than hold Kasim here until Inspector Lee arrives? He looked at the Asian Islamists who were watching the fight.

No, he shook his head. Let them watch as their beloved Imam gets his ass handed to him. He suppressed a smile. It might teach them something.

He heard a thud and a groan and turned in time to see Kasim recoil from another blow to his face. Blood was running freely down the Imam's face as

128

he backed away from his tormentor, holding his hands up and, Sean imagined, begging for mercy.

He didn't show any mercy to Bruce's mother, Sean thought. Why should he expect any now?

Bruce took a step toward the beaten man, raised his arm for another blow...

And Kasim ducked under that arm and ran for the back door.

"No you don't," Sean said, blocking the Imam's route to safety. "It's time to reap the whirlwind." He smashed a palm into the other man's face, flattening his nose and sending him backwards.

Into Bruce's waiting arms.

The big Asian smiled grimly and grabbed a handful of Kasim's shirt, holding him at arm's length while he prepared for another blow.

CHAPTER TWELVE

Kelly's cab pulled up in front of the mosque just as Inspector Lee's car did. His eyes widened as he looked at the ruined front of the place.

"What do you know about all this?" Lee asked as he exited his own car, not yet having seen the carnage.

"Not much more than you do," Kelly told him. "I know she was grabbed sometime this morning—I got a call instructing me to take the train to a certain station…"

"Then another call sending you somewhere else," the policeman nodded. "Standard."

"I was waiting for a train to take me to the second stop when I got a text and image from Piper," he pulled out his phone.

"Never mind," Lee winced and shook his head. "I've seen it."

"It looks like Bruce has already taken a hand," Kelly nodded toward the back of the silver van which was sticking out of the front door of the mosque like some metallic tongue. "Shall we join him?"

It wasn't easy to get inside. The van had smashed the wooden frame of the door outward, causing the roof to sag and lock the vehicle in place. Kelly and Inspector Lee had to work their way around the wreckage—a tight fit for the burly CIA man.

By the time they got inside, Bruce had knocked Kasim to the floor for the fourth time and was standing over the bleeding man, sweating and trying to decide what he should do next.

"Piper!" Kelly yelled as he saw the young agent standing a few feet behind the one-sided fight. "What's happening?"

"Not much," Sean told him. "I'm just letting Bruce here deal with the man who killed his mother."

"You're sure of that?" Inspector Lee asked.

"You saw the picture?"

Lee nodded.

"Then you know the answer." Sean bowed his head a bit. "I'm sorry."

"Where is she?"

"In the back," Sean nodded to the empty portal where the door had once stood. "Little room on the left."

"Any trouble with the natives?" Kelly asked.

"Not since I showed them I was serious about letting Bruce here do whatever he wanted to do." Sean tapped the gun holstered at the back of his belt and took a few steps toward the two. "They really didn't seem that enthusiastic in any event."

"I'll have to take them all in," Inspector Lee noted. "You too."

"You do what you have to do," Sean told the policeman. "I understand."

"Good." The Inspector pushed his way through the frozen-in-place congregants. "Show me where…"

At that exact instant, Kasim Rageah made his move, slamming a heel into his opponent's crotch and pushing himself upright.

He staggered toward the open door at the best speed he could manage, barely avoiding Bruce's reflexive grab for his foot.

"He's getting away!" Kelly shouted.

"He can't get far." Inspector Lee drew his gun and followed the man with Sean just a half-step behind.

"There's a door that leads outside just to the right," Sean told him. "We don't want him getting to that!"

"Don't worry," Lee's voice was grim as death itself. "I don't intend…"

They came into the Imam's office—and saw Kasim at his desk, yanking the top drawer open.

"He's going for the gun he has there," Sean told his companion. "But don't worry about it, I…"

The outside door burst open, revealing Frank Farrell, his pistol already drawn.

The disturbance drew Sean and Lee's attention away from the Imam for a split second, when they turned back, the man had gotten his hand around the heavy-caliber automatic and was raising it in the general direction of Sean and Inspector Lee.

"Don't shoot!" Sean yelled—but it was too late. Kasim Rageah's body trembled as bullets from the guns of Lee; Farrell; and the just-arrived Kelly hit him. He stood there for a long second, his eyes puzzled.

Then he fell to the floor, dead.

***

"His gun had no bullets," Sean told the others as they advanced on the body. "I removed them when I first arrived here."

"Pity," the tone of Lee's voice didn't match the word. "You said my wife was back there?" He nodded toward the curtained off room to one side of the broken door.

"Yeah," Sean nodded. "I pulled a blanket over her." He looked at Inspector Lee. "I'm sorry I didn't get here sooner."

The policeman nodded once as he walked toward the room, already knowing what he was going to find inside.

Sean was the only one close enough to hear his carefully-suppressed sob of agony.

***

"What the hell were you thinking of!" Farrell lashed out at Kelly as soon as they had returned to Universal Exports. "You have responsibilities here—you can't just go off..."

"He said he'd kill Mary."

"He did kill Mary!" Farrell responded. "And he'd have killed you too if Sean here hadn't gotten to him first."

"Maybe..." Sean put in.

"I'll get to you later," Farrell spat at him, eyes still angry. "You shouldn't have gone off without me! That's what partners are for!"

"But you were wounded and one of us had to stay here in case..."

"In case Ms. Liu showed up?" Farrell shook his head. "Well, she didn't and as far as I can tell, she and her little group are in the wind." He looked at Kelly. "Unless you know where their base of operations is located."

"Somewhere to the west..."

"Yeah," Farrell shook his head. "That's a lot of help—and in the meantime, CIA assets are getting killed all over the world." He looked at Sean. "If you check your tablet, I think you'll find that two more were disposed of today."

"Look, Frank." Sean spread out his hands. "Just what did you expect me to do? Let Kelly here go out there and get killed? I had to follow up and that mosque seemed the most logical place to find Mrs. Lee." He looked at the slumped form of Kelly. "We both recognized the voice on the phone."

"And you took action while the senior CIA representative went for a ride on the train." Farrell shook his head. "I wonder what his bosses would say about that!"

"Look," Kelly looked into Farrell's eyes, his own showing the deep sadness he was feeling. "When you work in a station like this for a long time, the people you work with begin to feel like family…"

"That's no reason to throw away your own life." Farrell shook his head. "Damn it, Brian, you know better!"

"Maybe I forgot," Kelly shook his head and looked at Sean. "Like I forget a lot of things…"

"Listen," Sean leaned forward, eyes on his partner. "We can go over all this later—for now, it's vital that we find Ms. Liu!"

"Why?" Farrell sneered. "Because you think she's 'hot'?"

"No," Sean shook his head. "Because I think she'll lead us to the people that stole the CIA paymaster information."

"And you have a way to find her?"

"Maybe," Sean nodded slowly. "We have her cell phone number—if it's turned on, I can find out where it is."

"And if it's not turned on?"

"I still have that IP address—it would be a slog but I think I can work out a way to triangulate its position." He looked at Farrell. "If we can't find Ms. Liu some other way."

"All right," Farrell nodded. "Try the phone first."

"Yes sir," Sean nodded and turned away, anxious to get out of the room before the real argument between Farrell and Kelly broke out.

CHAPTER THIRTEEN

"The price is the price," Ms. Liu told the man on the phone. "We do not give discounts of any kind." She listened for a long second, then nodded and spoke again: "Drop the agreed upon fee at the usual place. Once I have it in hand, I will inform my people that they may release the information to you." Another nod. "That will be satisfactory."

She cut the connection and looked around. The Aberdeen Boat Club was miles from the commune's home but the signals from the Boat Club and the nearby Marine Police Port Headquarters made it almost impossible for anyone to listen in on her cell phone conversations.

Although, she thought, the American NSA might be able to cut through all the static and find a single call.

That organization, however, had been crippled by a clever publicity campaign and pandering to the lowest elements of the American population.

It is almost too easy, she shook her head. The Americans are very predictable—and far too soft to give us any kind of difficulty in the world to come.

Ms. Liu smiled as she thought about that world—then turned and headed up the road. She had plenty of time to get to Che Kung Temple and the money that would be waiting for her there.

***

All right, Sean rubbed his eyes tiredly. Her phone was definitely active for a while. He'd found indications of its sim card near the Hong Kong docks—but the electronic activity there was so intense, it was hard to find its precise location before the signal disappeared entirely.

She turned the phone off once she finished her conversation. Sean realized. After holding that conversation in a spot where her phone would be difficult to trace.

It was going to be very hard to find her if she was always that careful.

There must be another way. He pulled the IP address up on his computer and looked at it for a long minute, then glanced at the time. It's just past eight o'clock at night here, he thought. Which means it's eight in the morning in Washington. He pulled out his phone and tapped out a number. I hate to do this but, he shrugged. I can't see another way.

The phone on the other end began to ring.

***

It was nearly ten in the morning by the time Sean joined Farrell and Kelly in the office the next day. He asked the two senior agents to join him in Kelly's office, refusing to tell them why until he had a little privacy.

Farrell was worried about the way the youngster looked. Sean looks tired, he thought. Am I working him too hard on this case? Should I order him to take a break?

Sean did look tired—he had every right to because he was, in fact, working far harder than his partner dreamed.

It had taken nearly four hours to get the answer he had called Washington for and then had taken several hours more to find the last piece of the

137

puzzle. Then, and only then, did he allow himself to get some sleep.

Now he was face to face with the two most senior agents on the site--and he was dreading what he had to say.

It's not going to get easier if I wait; he knew that to be a fact, even as he knew how each of the two men in the office with him would react to what he had discovered. It will help us get to the bottom of this whole mess. He glanced at Kelly, the burly station chief. Even if it that means destroying his career...

He straightened in his chair and looked at Farrell. "I found the location of the IP address through which the hackers got into the CIA paymaster system."

"That's great!" Farrell smiled. "I thought you didn't have the gear you needed to find it here."

"I don't, I was forced to ask for help." he shrugged. "Help from the FBI Cyber team."

"And they gave it to you?"

Sean smiled. "I mentioned Mary Max's name and their agents were practically falling over themselves to find what I wanted."

"So where did the hack come from?" Kelly leaned forward. "Was it Ms. Liu's 'Commune' or some other group?"

"I didn't say I knew who did the actual hack," Sean told him. "I said I knew where the computer used tied into the internet."

"We know the approximate location of the commune," Kelly gestured with one hand. "We can find it easily enough."

"Maybe," Sean shook his head. "But we won't have to worry about that."

"Why not?"

"Because the hack came from right here," Sean slapped a hand down on Kelly's desk. "Inside this office!"

Kelly and Farrell stared at him as if he had grown two heads.

CHAPTER FOURTEEN

"All right," Victoria Liu used a cheap burner cell phone she'd purchased at a stand near the train station for her next call. "I understand," she smiled. "The information will be made available as soon as your payment is received." She looked around, judging the region around her.

Yes, she thought, seeing a familiar structure to the west. That would be so perfect!

"Leave the money—as specified—by the bronze statue of Walt and Mickey in the central hub of Hong Kong Disneyland." She nodded once. "You have three hours—and do not try to tell us that someone else picked the payment up—we will be watching."

She listened to the stammered objections from the man on the other end of the line.

"Three hours," she shook her head. "We will be awaiting your payment."

She clicked the phone off and tossed it into a nearby trash container. This is getting too complicated and dangerous, she looked around, alert for signs of anyone watching her. It's only a matter of time before Kelly and his friends in the CIA realize exactly what we're doing. She shook her head and headed across the road, pulling out a second burner phone she had purchased earlier at a different shop as she did so. After that happens, they'll do everything they can to find us, she hopped onto the curb as a cab beeped its horn at her and stopped while she sent a text to a specific number. We'll need to disappear before that happens. She smiled. Maybe we'll go to Paris— I'm told it's really nice in the springtime.

Her smile widened as she turned and motioned for the next cab on the street to pick her up. Of course we could just eliminate them. She climbed in. But I'd hate to do that—Mr. Kelly's been so helpful. A smile drifted across her lips. And that new agent—Sean—he looked interesting—like someone I'd like to get to know...

She got the confirmation she was waiting for just as the car pulled away, heading for the Chinese equivalent of the 'Happiest Place on Earth'.

***

"I tried to trace Ms. Liu's phone yesterday," Sean told the others, avoiding the sudden scepticism in their gaze. "And found a slight trace—down near one of the docks." He shook his head. "Nothing we could follow up on."

"I don't care about that," Kelly snarled. "Tell us why you think the hack was done through my office computer!"

"Okay," Sean took a deep breath. "After the phone trace failed, I decided to concentrate my efforts on the IP Address," he looked into the CIA man's eyes. "At that point, I didn't think we were going to be getting any help from Ms. Liu and her 'Commune'."

Farrell nodded agreement.

"I just don't have the tools to track an IP address from here—so I called the FBI Cyber division and explained my problem. They informed me that they had been tracing the OPM hack and had built a map of other IP addresses in the immediate area." He made a gesture. "By sheer luck, one of those addresses was the one I've been searching for."

"And?" Kelly demanded.

"They sent me a copy of the map and I was able to pinpoint the position of the address in question." Sean met his eyes. "It came from inside this building."

"It could have been one of the other tenants," Kelly sputtered. "There are nearly ninety other businesses in this building."

"I thought of that," Sean nodded. "So I decided to take a closer look at your computer." He held up a blockish piece of plastic. "I found this."

"What is it?" Farrell asked.

"It's a computer chip," Sean held it higher. "More accurately, it is a 'GPRS Chip'.

"What the hell is that?"

"GPRS chips," Sean told him. "Are used to manage the sessions and tunneling protocols necessary for them to operate on a GSM network." He looked at the chip. "This one has both a memory cache and a management unit to handle two-way communications."

"Two way?"

Sean nodded. "Whoever put this in your computer was able to use it to acquire a continuous flow of IP packets."

"Talk English!" Kelly yelled.

"Simply put," Sean looked at him. "Somebody put this into one of your computer's communications nodes, than, with their own computer, they were able to hack into the CIA mainframe using your IP, codes, and clearances.

Once inside, they gained access to the Paymaster programs and copied the information from them—through that communications node—to their hard drive." He shook his head. "They copied everything they needed and, when they were done, just shut down the hack, packed up their computer, and walked away, assuming that it would be years before this little beauty was found."

"But how...?"

"I assume that someone gained access to your computer for a long enough period to plant this device—the rest was done remotely."

"Captain?" Farrell's eyes were on the CIA station chief now.

"The computer is password protected," he protested. "And no one gets into this office without being cleared..."

"No one?" Sean bit his lip. "I seem to remember you being pretty chummy with one of your secretaries the day we arrived in Hong Kong."

"Linda?" Kelly shook his head. "We did a full background check on her, there's no way..."

"Where is she now?" Farrell asked. "I don't remember seeing her for the past few days."

"She called in sick yesterday--said she would be back on Monday." Kelly looked from Farrell to Sean. "She didn't have access to this office! She couldn't have ..."

"You and Linda wouldn't have been doing a little 'after-hours' work on occasion, would you?" Farrell asked. "I seem to remember that you have a bit of a weakness for a pretty face..."

Kelly shook his head, thinking. "She was never alone! I was with her..." He stopped and looked at

Sean. "How long would it take to install this chip of yours?"

"If the installer knew what they were doing," he shrugged. "Maybe three or four minutes."

"I can't believe..."

"Who told you about Ms. Liu and her people," Farrell suddenly asked. "Did you get their information from an external source?"

Kelly looked at him.

"Linda told you, didn't she?"

Kelly nodded stiffly.

"What else has she told you? Who else has she introduced into the office?"

"No one." Kelly shook his head. "No one at all."

"Kek..."

"I'm telling you the truth—Linda and I might have had a little fling but she never—never—brought anyone else into the office. She told me about some people—like Liu—but she never brought them here without me being there as well."

"How many did you bring in," Sean asked quietly. "On your own."

"No one! Aside from Ms. Liu, she never gave me a name interesting enough..." He stopped short. "There was one other person," he looked around. "We had a problem with the air conditioning last summer and she suggested we use a cousin of hers..."

"Check the vents," Farrell jumped to his feet. "Be careful!"

Sean headed for the vent on the far side of the office—it was in the lower part of the wall just behind Kelly's desk. He dropped to his knees,

144

pulled a pencil light out of his pocket, and shined it through the latticework grate, looking for anything out of the ordinary.

What he saw shocked him enough that he backed away and bumped into Kelly's desk chair ...

CHAPTER FIFTEEN

The pick-up went just as planned; the client never even glanced in Ms. Liu's direction as he slid the payment carefully into place. She played it safe, however, and waited while he turned and headed down 'Main Street' toward the park entrance, waiting until ...

Her newest burner phone, purchased as she entered the Park, rang.

"Yes?" She answered, and then smiled. "All right—I'll get the package." She listened to the reply, then: "No, not just yet." She walked across the street and picked up the parcel of bills their client had placed alongside the bronze statue of Walt Disney and Mickey Mouse. "While we're here, I'd like to take a few minutes to talk." Ms. Liu looked at the castle across from her. "Let's meet in front of my favorite ride," she nodded at the response. "That's the one—I'll see you there in a few minutes."

She stuffed the parcel of money into her bag, dropped the phone into a convenient garbage can, and strolled across the central plaza, heading for the rendezvous point—and some fun.

***

Mystic Manor is one of the most technologically advanced attractions at any Disney park. It is set in the home of Lord Henry Mystic, an explorer and collector of ancient artefacts.

146

"Do we have to do this again?" Linda asked as she met Ms. Liu at the start of the ride queue. "I mean, that music…"

"I love the music," Ms. Liu told her. "Besides, it's dark and cool in there." She smiled. "And we have things to discuss."

"Somebody at the CIA found the GPRS chip," Linda told her as they reached the front of the ride and boarded their vehicle. "They're going to figure the whole thing out pretty quickly now."

"That's all right," Ms. Liu tapped her bag. "I think we've taken in just about as much as we can." She looked at her companion. "It's time to get out of here." She smiled. "I've been considering travelling to Paris…"

"There are a lot of Muslim crazies in France," Linda brushed a stray lock back from her forehead. "We could still make a little money out of our data stash."

"It's always money with you!" Ms. Liu watched, eyes wide with delight, as Lord Mystic's mischievous pet monkey, Albert, began to fiddle with the magical music box that, Ms. Liu knew, would soon bring any number of inanimate objects to life. "Why don't you ever just want to have some fun?"

She giggled as the music started.

"I got to have all the fun I could stand with that bastard Kelly," Linda noted, her face reflecting her tone. "That was enough for a while."

"Come on," Ms. Liu ran a soft hand down her partner's cheek. "Just relax for a little while—at least while we're in here!"

"Maybe for a little while," Linda smiled and gave her partner a tender kiss...

***

"You're right," Farrell stared at the object beyond the grate. "That is an explosive device." He leaned closer. "Looks like a Claymore." He turned and regarded the room beyond the grate. "If that went off, it would have torn anyone at the desk to ribbons." He smiled at Kelly. "They really didn't like you, Captain."

"Don't call me that!"

"All right," Farrell smiled. "We're going to need some tools. Do you have a screwdriver?" He looked at the corner of the grate. "Straight edge should work."

"Not here," Kelly headed for the door. "Back in the utilities room." He pushed the door open and disappeared into the offices beyond.

"Think he's going to come back?" Sean asked.

"I'm not sure." Farrell pulled his own pocket knife out and opened the built-in screwdriver blade. "But I'm not going to wait."

"That's not just a normal claymore," Sean asked. "Is it?"

"Nope." Farrell got one screw free, put it on the floor next to the grate. "There something attached to it—I'm thinking it's a remote detonator."

"Radio controlled."

"Probably goes through that chip you have."

"I disengaged the two-way radio system—nobody can send a signal through this now."

"Good," Farrell placed a second screw next to the first. "Because I'd hate to be doing this if Linda

148

happens to discover that Kelly gave her chlamydia!" He began working on the third screw. "She might be pissed off enough to set this off."

The third screw joined the others.

"Now," Farrell turned to the final screw. "If this thing doesn't have a tremblor switch…"

The fourth screw came out cleanly.

"What now?" Sean asked.

"Now we carefully slide that thing out of here…" He reached in, got a firm grasp on either side of the Claymore. "I'd like to cut away the ductwork and do this from the side but I don't think the neighboring offices would be too happy about that." He pulled the Claymore toward him. "No tricks there," he slid it carefully out of the duct. "I guess whoever planted this didn't have much time."

He put the Claymore on the floor, wiped a bit of sweat off his brow.

"Captain owes us for that," he said. "I'll have to add it to the list."

"What now?"

"First let's disarm the radio detonator." Farrell carefully stood up. "Your turn, I think."

Sean allowed his partner to slide by him then took the other man's place on the floor. A quick examination showed him that the extra unit on the rear of the device was, indeed, a radio detonator.

He bent for a closer look. "This thing is set at the same frequency as the chip," he looked at Farrell. "It's safe enough."

"What if someone uses a radio or walkie at the same frequency?"

"Didn't think of that," Sean bent back to the device. "Let me borrow your knife."

He took Farrell's blade, folded the screwdriver back into its place and extended the larger knife blade. "There're two wires attaching the radio unit to the power source," he got closer still. "Red should be power, black should be ground."

"You sure?"

"I guess I'll have to be." Sean slid the blade under the red wire and, with a quick movement, cut through it. "Yep," he smiled. "Red was power."

"So the thing is harmless for the moment." Farrell helped his partner to his feet. "We're going to have to find something to use in place of the safety that whoever planted this thing removed."

"Paper clip?"

"Not thick enough." Farrell began opening desk drawers. "Has to be something sturdier..."

"How about this?" Sean reached in and withdrew a leather collar with a series of large rings around the outside face. "That ring should be thick enough..."

"Let's see if we can get it off and bend it."

They could—and did—and soon had it in place. The Claymore was safe for the moment.

"I didn't see any large dogs around here." Sean said as he tossed the collar onto Kelly's desk and sank into one of the chairs."

"The Captain doesn't have a dog." Farrell found a bottle of scotch in a corner cabinet and poured two stiff drinks. "That collar was for another kind of pet." He handed a glass to Sean. "Like the missing secretary, Linda."

"Oh," Sean pursed his lips as he thought about that. "Oh..."

CHAPTER SIXTEEN

"Want to go around again?" Ms. Liu asked her partner as the ride came to its end.

"Not right now," the former secretary looked at her companion. "Right now I want to get back to the apartment and make plans." She tapped the bag at Ms. Liu's side. "We've got to think about the future—and what we're going to do."

"Spoilsport!" Ms. Liu stuck out her tongue but followed her partner away from the Manor and back down Main Street toward the outside world.

"I love this place," the hacker said as they went through the gates. "It helps me forget about everything outside."

"There's a Disneyland in Paris," Linda pointed out. "Maybe we should move there."

"Do we have enough?"

"I think so." Linda smiled. "And if we set off the little surprise we left in Mr. Kelly's office…"

"You want to kill them?"

"I want to kill one of them." The former secretary's face went hard. "It would make it a lot easier for me to move if I knew he was gone."

"Okay," Ms. Liu nodded. "Let's get somewhere within radio range."

"We can't just use the computer?"

"No," she shook her head. "I told you that the young guy—Sean—found our chip." She shrugged. "I'm sure he's turned it off by now."

"Okay," Linda moved toward the train station. "We'll work our way back into town."

151

"And when we get there, we'll need a walkie talkie or something like it."

"Lots of stores carry that kind of thing." Linda smiled. "We can have an early dinner and watch the carnage when we set it off."

"You have a really nasty streak inside that pretty head, don't you?"

"I didn't before I met Mr. Kelly." Linda's smile disappeared. "He brought out the worst in me."

"Forget about him," Ms. Liu put her arm over her partner's shoulder. "Just think about Paris and all the wonderful things we're going to be able to buy there!"

Linda smiled and, arm in arm, the two girls climbed the stairs to the train station.

* * *

"Will this work?" Kelly asked as he stepped back into the office, a screwdriver in his hand.

"A little late," Sean drawled.

"Indeed," Farrell. "We've already disarmed the explosive." He looked around. "Which I assume you knew..."

"Security cameras on the wall over there," Sean pointed. "I assume there's a monitor on one of the secretary's desks."

"Are you trying to imply that I hid out while you two were working on that Claymore?" Kelly frowned.

"Hell," Farrell shook his head. "We're not implying anything—we're simply stating a fact." He looked Kelly in the eye. "You ran out of this office as soon as you realized there was a danger and only came back when that danger was over."

He nodded toward the security camera. "The camera only tells us that you were keeping an eye on things."

"I resent that!" Kelly drew himself up to his full height. "You know that..."

"I know that you've been running away from danger for the past ten years." Farrell shook his head sadly. "I only wish I knew why."

"Let's talk about that later," Sean put the Claymore on Kelly's desk. "Right now, I'd really like to see about getting some food." He looked at the two older men. "With friend Kasim out of the way, I think we can safely go to one of the nearby restaurants."

"Good idea," Farrell's eyes didn't leave Kelly. "It'll give the three or us a chance to have a talk without any other ears," he glanced at the camera. "Or eyes, paying attention."

"Okay," Kelly glared at Farrell. "I'll tell my people that we're going out for a while, but you should know..."

"What should I know, Captain?" Farrell met Kelly—glare for glare. "Should I know that you're an outright coward? Should I know that you'll run at the first sign of danger?" He moved a step closer, his chest almost touching the other man. "Tell me—just what is it I should know that I haven't already figured out?"

Kelly started to say something—then caught himself and backed away.

"Yeah," Farrell nodded. "That's what I thought." He pushed the burly station chief out of his way and headed for the elevator. "I'll see you downstairs." He glanced back. "The air is cleaner there."

As the door closed behind Farrell, Kelly turned to Sean, eyes pleading. "Sean, no matter what Frank says, I'm not a coward. Really, I…"

"Frank's right," the younger agent said, shouldering past the station chief and heading for the door. "There is a bad smell in here." He looked at the burly man. "We'll meet you downstairs." He caught the other man's eye. "Don't make us wait too long."

Then he was gone and Brian Kelly was alone, staring at the door of his own office.

***

At almost the same instant, Ms. Liu and Linda were getting off their train amid the maze of buildings that formed the center of Hong Kong.

"We'll want to eat in a place that overlooks the AIA center," Ms. Liu pointed out.

"You're sure the little radio set you purchased outside Disneyland is going to work?" The other woman replied. "Perhaps we should stop in one of the electronic shops and get something more powerful?"

"This little walkie talkie unit will work just fine," Ms. Liu tapped the box that was partially visible at the top of her tote bag. "I only have to adjust the frequency a little bit."

"If you're sure it'll work," Linda pointed up the street. "Why don't we go to Peking Garden?" She smiled. "It's one of Mr. Kelly's favorite places to eat." She grinned. "We can charge the meal to his account."

154

"You are evil!" Ms. Liu put an arm around her friend. "Let's go to Peking Garden and watch the fireworks."

They strode down the street, arm in arm, Linda smiling as she envisioned the destruction of Kelly, his toys, and the office that held them.

***

"You have to cool off a little," Sean told his partner as he joined him in the AIA lobby. "You know what he's like—you can't expect him to change…"

"He has changed." Farrell turned toward the younger man, eyes sad. "When I first met Brian Kelly, he was absolutely fearless—ready to tackle anything, no matter what." He shook his head. "He was a brilliant soldier—never failed to complete his mission…"

"Sounds like my Dad."

"He was a lot like your Dad—but while your Dad was one of the best shots I ever saw—and a brilliant field leader, Kelly did his best work without ever using a weapon."

"How does that work?"

"Kelly was in Marine Recon—they get the same training as the Navy's SEAL's but instead of being used in combat roles, Marine Recon scouts enemy positions way out in front of their units." Farrell shook his head. "The best Marine Recon troops consider it a failure if they actually have to shoot at anything—means they screwed up somewhere along the line."

"Sounds hard."

"It is—and Kelly was one of the best. I recruited him on a mission in Helmand Province—

we were trying to retrieve an asset who was way beyond our lines." Farrell shook his head. "Kelly went in alone—and came out with the asset," his eyes met Sean's. "He never fired a shot."

"Sounds like someone who'd make a great spy."

"That's what I thought. So I brought him into the CIA—not as a shooter like your father, but as a regular intelligence analyst. It turned out that he had a real talent for languages—so we sent him to the old Army language school at the Presidio—nice place," he shrugged. "Gone now..."

"So he went to the language school..." Sean prodded.

"Oh," Farrell shook away his memories of the Presidio. "Yeah—he did well in the school, mastered three different Chinese dialects—not an easy thing to do. We sent him to a monitoring station on Okinawa and he did some good work there." He looked at the younger agent. "From there he worked with me on some jobs in Syria—which is how he met your father."

"Dad never talked about anyone like him."

"You Dad never really took a shine to him." Farrell smiled. "Robert was a very straightforward man—he always spoke his mind and wore his heart on his sleeve."

"And Kelly doesn't."

"Not when he's on a job." Farrell sucked at his lower lip, and then continued. "When the Libya thing went bad and your dad and his team were killed, Kelly got promoted and sent to the China Desk at Langely and later, to the station here."

"Because he obeyed orders," Sean's voice was cold. "And left my father to die."

"It wasn't that simple." The burly man's voice came from behind them. "I had my men ready to go—orders or no orders," he met Sean's eyes as the youngster turned toward him. "But something happened—something that kept me from doing anything at all."

"What was that?" Farrell growled.

"I had…" Kelly shrugged. "Call it a mutiny. Five of my men refused to leave the annex—flat-out told me they weren't going to disobey headquarters for any reason." His eyes searched Farrell's. "A guy named Mosby was the ringleader. For a moment, I thought that if I could just get him to move, get him to take action…" Kelly shook his head. "Before I made a decision, he had a gun pointed at my head and that was that." He frowned. "We defended the Annex—kept everyone there alive—but there was never a chance to do anything else." He shut his eyes. "They never let me do anything else."

"Why didn't you tell us that at the time—report the mutiny?"

"How could I?" Kelly sighed. "What was I going to say? That my men wouldn't obey me when I told them to disobey orders from higher headquarters?" He shook his head. "No, there was nothing I could do. Nothing but move on to something else"

He looked at Farrell. I was ashamed of what I didn't do—I had dreams, nightmares…" He shook his head. "You wouldn't have had any trouble getting those men to follow you, but I did. I

157

couldn't get it done. Couldn't even bring myself to fight them…"

Kelly bowed his head and stared down at the floor. "My confidence was shot. I couldn't handle conflict of any kind—I had to back off on arguments, avoid confrontations." He smiled wanly. "It even affected my sex life—I was even afraid there…"

"So you started playing bondage games…"

"It was the only way for me to feel strong and in charge."

""Have you talked to anyone else about this?"

"You mean my bosses back at Langley?" He shook his head. "Hell no, they'd have me on the first plane out of here and I'd be unemployed a week later!"

"I don't know what to think about this…" Farrell rubbed his eyes tiredly. "I'm going to need some time..."

"Maybe we can talk over dinner," Kelly pleaded. "You two said you were hungry—I'll take you to my favorite place—it's not far from here."

"I guess it'll be safe enough," Sean drawled. "Now that Kasim is dead." He looked at Kelly. "What's the restaurant called?"

"The Peking Garden." Kelly smiled. "Food is great and it has a wonderful view of the city."

"All right," Sean put his hand on Farrell's shoulder and urged him out the door. "The Peking Garden it will be!"

The three men exited the AIA center and headed down the block…

CHAPTER SEVENTEEN

The Maître d' recognized Linda from past visits and put her and her companion, Ms. Liu, at a table near the window—just as they requested.

"Will Mr. Kelly be joining you?" He asked as he placed menus in front of the two girls.

"He might drop in," Linda smiled at the concept.

"I hope he does," the Maître d' bowed and turned back to his podium at the front of the restaurant.

"You are so evil," Ms. Liu told her companion, giggling.

"I was only telling the truth," Linda's grew as she spoke. "Parts of him might drop into this area; after all, his office is right there." She pointed out the window at the mass of the AIA Center.

"I guess," Ms. Liu sighed. "When do you want to do it?"

"Let's get a drink first," Linda signaled for a waitress. "We should drink a toast—after all, without Mr. Kelly, we wouldn't be travelling to Paris together, now would we?"

"Probably not." Ms. Liu sat silent while her companion ordered two glasses of white wine. "No champagne?" She asked.

"Later perhaps," Linda made a small gesture. "I want to be completely sober when we eliminate that pig."

"As you please," Ms. Liu took the small transmitter out of her bag and fiddled with the frequency settings. "That should be about right..." She looked out the window, estimated the distance between their table and Kelly's office. "We should be well within range..."

"Quiet!" Linda nodded toward the approaching waitress.

Both girls stayed silent as they received their glasses of wine.

"Are you ready to order yet?" The woman asked them.

"Give us a moment," Linda made a tiny gesture with her finger. "We have something we want to do first."

The waitress nodded and moved to the next table in her sector.

"Okay," Linda lifted her glass. "A toast!" She looked at her partner. "To the end of oppression!"

"The end of oppression," Ms. Liu tapped rims with the other girl. "And the continuation of a beautiful friendship." 'She held up the transmitter. "On three," she put her finger on the 'SEND' button. "One...Two..."

"THREE! She pushed the button down as hard as she could and turned to look at the AIA center, waiting for the explosion she knew had to come.

Nothing happened.

"What's wrong?" Linda leaned forward, suddenly concerned. "Why didn't it go off?"

"This transmitter must not have enough range," she studied the frequency settings, made sure the connections were secure. "You might have been right about that."

"What can we do?"

"There's an electronics store less than a block from here," Ms. Liu stood up, grabbing her bag. "Order some appetizers for us and I'll go and buy something a bit stronger than this toy," she put the transmitter down. "I won't be long." She gave her companion a kiss on the cheek. "I'm just as anxious to have this over with as you are."

"All right," Linda bit her lower lip, suddenly concerned. "Don't take too long."

"I won't," she smiled and gave her friend another kiss. "I promise."

Then she was gone, hurrying out of the restaurant toward the crowded street beyond.

The store she wanted was just a block or so away—almost across the busy street from the AIA building. The streets were crowded and Ms. Liu had to push her way through the mass, slowing her down. Thus she had gone less than a half block when she saw a flash of unusual movement across the street.

Right in front of the AIA complex.

Those are very tall men! She thought, struggling to slow down for a better look as the crowd pushed her along. I wonder...

The light changed and the three men moved in her direction. A glimpse of his face told her that it was, in fact, Mr. Kelly accompanied by the two new agents from the United States.

Crap! She fought her way away from the curb and slid into the doorway of a bank, eyes wide. I wonder where they're going? She watched as they reached her side of the street and turned in the direction from which she had just come. If they go into the Peking Gardens and find Linda...

She grabbed a cell phone from her bag and punched in a number from memory. I hope they're there, she watched the three men cut through the crowd, moving without apparent effort. Because if they're not...

She stepped out of the doorway and followed Kelly and the others up the street. I don't know what we'll do!

***

Linda was just sipping the last of her wine when her cell phone rang.

"Hello." She listened for a second, her eyes widening. "They're coming here!" She looked around, saw movement near the doorway. "All right—I'll try to keep out of sight—I'll go to the Ladies Room," she nodded. "Let me know when you expect them to arrive."

She jabbed at the 'OFF' button as Kelly came through the front door of the restaurant and smiled at the Maître d'.

He'll bring him over here, she knew. I've got to move!

Linda stood and walked toward the Ladies Room that stood in one corner of the restaurant. She fought the urge to turn her head and check to see where Kelly was.

She knew that would be foolish and might get her caught.

Instead, she moved between tables with the grace of a champion halfback and gained the safety of the toilet with seconds to spare.

***

162

"Mr. Kelly!" The Maître d' smiled as the tall CIA chief came into the Restaurant. "It's a pleasure to see you! Miss Linda said…"

"Linda?" Kelly frowned at him. "Linda Chou is here?"

"I seated her and another leady less then fifteen minutes ago." The Maître d' shrugged. "They wanted a very specific table—one that overlooked the AIA building." He raised a hand and motioned for a waitress to join them. "Chin, you have the two young ladies?"

"They've only ordered wine and appetizers so far," she said. "They seem to be waiting for something."

"Can you show these gentlemen to their table?"

"Of course," she gestured. "This way."

A moment later Kelly and the others were at the table so recently vacated by Linda and Ms. Liu.

"They were here just a moment ago," the waitress looked around. "Perhaps they've gone to the Lady's Room…"

"It's all right," Kelly smiled and slipped a bank note into the waitress's hand. "We'll wait for them right here."

"Yes sir," the woman nodded. "Can I get you anything while you wait?"

"Just some water," Kelly looked at the others. "We'll order when they join us."

"Yes sir." The woman nodded and turned back to her other tables. There's something going on there, she thought. Something I don't think I want to be a part of…

She hurried away without a look back.

***

"Do you think it's really her?" Sean asked, settling into a seat that put his back to one of the windows. "I mean, what are the odds?"

"I don't know why she would come here," Kelly responded, taking a seat that gave him a view of the front door. "But Mr. Chiu," he nodded toward the Maître d' "knows her well. If he says she was here," Kelly shrugged. "Then she was certainly here."

"And someone was with her," Farrell pointed out. "Another woman." He looked at his two companions. "Ms. Liu?"

"That would be a bit of a stretch…"

"No," Sean shook his head. "It makes perfect sense! Think about it—if Linda and Ms. Liu were working together all along…"

"It would explain the hack and the bomb!"

"It would explain everything!" Sean looked at Kelly's face. "Two women who were completely trusted. Imagine how easy that made the whole thing."

"I can't believe…"

"Look." Farrell kept his voice low but injected a note of urgency into the single word. "Check out that man just outside the door." He nodded in that direction. "He's stopped in that spot twice since we were seated…"

"He's just looking for a friend," Kelly put in. "Or seeing if there's an open table."

"Maybe." Farrell shrugged. "But I have a feeling…"

"Look to his right," Sean put in. "He's got some friends joining him."

"See?" Kelly told Farrell. "He was just waiting for his group to get together. Now they'll come in and..."

"One of them has a gun," Sean said quietly.

"You're wrong," Farrell told him. "They all have guns."

"Crap," Kelly said, blood draining from his face.

"You know," Sean touched the pistol holstered at the small of his back. "I think I hate the restaurants in Hong Kong." He left his hand on the grip. "I haven't actually eaten dinner in one of them yet!"

***

Jason Yuetwoh was well-known in the Hong Kong community as a 'tough guy'. Had Bruce Lee still been around, Yuetwoh would have challenged him to a fight and been shocked had he lost.

With Bruce Lee dead, Yuetwoh had been forced to put his 'talents' to use through very different outlets. He and his gang competed with several established Hong Kong Tongs, fighting them for territory and protection money from the merchants in those territories.

His parents had been friends with the parents of Victoria Liu and when they were both students, she had helped tutor him in subjects in which he was having difficulties.

While she prepared for college, he ended up in the 'Commerce Stream', an educational path intended to help him find a vocation.

It did. A year later, Jason Yuetwoh was a member of one of the many gangs that plagued the city. By the time Ms. Liu graduated from college,

Jason Yuetwoh was the leader of a large gang—one that controlled several blocks at the outer edges of Hong Kong.

Yuetwoh, no matter how high he rose, never forgot his friends and when Ms. Liu encountered difficulties rising through the ranks of Hong Kong techies, her friend found her a place in a commune of hackers—a commune she came to dominate and, until quite recently, lead.

When she had called him and explained the danger to her from Kelly and his friends, the young gang leader had been happy to lend a hand— particularly when she told him how big the price the local Muslim extremists had put on the CIA station chief's head.

That had brought him on the run and now he— and four of his men—were pushing into the Peking Gardens, determined to take care of the roundeye who was giving the girl their boss described as his 'little sister' such trouble.

They were glaring as they advanced on the table that held Kelly and his two companions...

**

"So what do we do?" Sean asked. "I don't want to start another gunfight." He looked around. "There are too many innocents who might get hurt."

"I'm not sure what else we can do," Farrell answered. "The only way out is past them."

"We might be able to get out through the restrooms." Kelly nodded toward the doors at the rear of the room. "Back there."

"Run?" Sean shook his head. "If we try that, they'll just shoot us in the back!"

"I don't know what else we can do."

"I do." Sean stood and faced the five thugs. "Translate for me."

Kelly started to stand up, already half-turned toward the restrooms.

Farrell caught him by the arm and pushed him back into his seat. "Translate for the kid," he hissed into the other's ear.

"Which one of you is in charge?" Sean called out, eyes wandering over the faces of the men at the front of the restaurant.

That one, Sean realized as Kelly translated his challenge--it wasn't hard to read the body language of this group.

I might have guessed, Sean thought, watching the leader's eyes as they weighed him. He was the first one here—probably casing the joint before making a move. Sean wondered how they had learned that Kelly was here—he assumed that this was just another attempt on the CIA Chief's life, never thinking that there might be more to it than that.

"Are you afraid to speak?" He called out, hearing Kelly's Cantonese echo behind him. "I thought you boys were supposed to be tough."

"Watch your mouth, Roundeye!" The leader said in more or less understandable English as he took a long step forward." I fear no man!"

"Prove it," Sean looked into the other man's eyes. "Fight me—alone—without guns or other weapons."

"You?" Yuetwoh barked a laugh. "You want to fight me?"

"I see you do understand English," Sean said loudly enough for the whole restaurant to hear. "Do I have to explain the concept of fighting?"

"You'll pay for that!" Yuetwoh muttered.

"Movie bad-guy dialogue 101," Sean smiled. "Probably the only schooling you ever got."

"Bastard!" The gang leader yelled—and charged right at Sean, leading with a roundhouse kick that he had used to down many opponents in the past.

It didn't down Sean—in fact, it didn't even touch him. The young agent had been expecting just such a move, assuming that the gang leader would want to show off his strength and prowess against this seemingly-helpless foe.

There was only one problem. Sean was many things--but he had never been anything like helpless...

He deflected the kick with an arm block, than glided under it, moving in close and flashing a lightning-quick open-handed blow into his opponent's jaw.

Teeth splintered at the force of the blow.

"Who..." Yuetwoh spat out the broken remnants of those teeth along with a gob of bloody saliva. "Who are you?"

"Nobody," Sean stood on the balls of his feet, ready for anything. "Just a tourist in this fair city trying to get some dinner."

"You..." The gang leader didn't say another word, he just moved with all the speed he had while he swung a long, looping right fist toward his opponent's head.

Sean ducked beneath the blow and, while his opponent tried to regain his balance, again stepped in close and landed two thunderous blows against the other man's chest--and a third, even harder strike, to his face.

Yuetwoh staggered backwards.

"Give it up," Sean told him. "I'm not going to let you get Mr. Kelly."

"I don't want Mr. Kelly anymore," the gang leader grabbed his broken nose between thumb and forefinger and pulled, snapping it more or less straight. "I want you! I want you dead!"

He reached for his gun.

Sean had been expecting just such a move. He was close enough to grab the other man's right wrist with his own left hand as he pivoted and drove a carefully aimed elbow strike into the other's condyle—the moveable joint between the mandible and the cranium part of the skull.

Bones broke as the side of the gang leader's jaw shattered under the force of the blow. Yuetwoh moaned and sagged against Sean who quietly removed the gun from the other's limp hand before dropping him, unconscious, to the floor.

"He'll need a doctor," Sean said as he turned toward Farrell and Kelly.

And hurriedly ducked as his partner raised his pistol right into Sean's face and pulled the trigger.

CHAPTER EIGHTEEN

I didn't want this! Ms. Liu thought as the window beside her spider-webbed under the impact of a 9mm bullet. *I didn't want any innocent people killed! I told Jason...*

She sighed. Jason was down, and there was nothing she could do to stop the gunfire—but there was one thing she could do.

"Linda!" She whispered into the cell phone when her partner answered. "You've got to get out now! While everyone is busy!" She ducked as another stray round hit the window, shattering it. "And be careful! There's a lot of gunfire!"

She heard a quick assent from her friend before the phone clicked off. *I hope she makes it;* Ms. Liu thought as she huddled behind what cover the metal around the doorway gave her. *If she doesn't,* she saw a volley of shots ring out. *I'm not sure what I'm going to do...*

***

Kelly was impressed by how easily young Piper handled the Chinese tough. Farrell had told him that the elder Piper had taught his son all kinds of martial arts while the boy was young but actually seeing him in action...

He's as fast as his father was, Kelly thought. *And just as deadly.* He shook his head as the youngster disabled his opponent and dropped him to the floor before turning to his partner for an opinion on what to do next. *I wish...*

170

"Look out!" Farrell yelled as he whipped his pistol up and fired it right through the space Piper had occupied just a moment before.

Kelly heard a "YELP" as one of the remaining gang members went down—then all hell broke loose.

Crap! The CIA chief shook his head as Farrell up-ended the table and took refuge behind it. I don't know if Inspector Lee is going to be able to cover another one of these up! Kelly tried to see where young Piper was but he couldn't really see anything beyond the edges of the table and didn't want to stick his head up too beyond its cover.

I should do something to help the boy, he thought. It might make up for what happened to his father. Kelly wasn't sure if Farrell had actually believed his story, but right now, it didn't really matter. Sean is out there, Kelly drew his own weapon. If I move now...

A bullet hit the table just to his right—and blew right through leaving a half-inch hole in its place.

And left Kelly frozen in place, shivering.

That could have killed me, he realized, drawing back. I can't go out there! He saw Farrell pop up to fire several shots. I can't!

He looked around. The restaurant was a study in chaos with people crouching down, crying, shouting, and, in some cases, making a run for a place of safety...

I've got to get out of here! Kelly began crawling as fast as he could toward the back of the room—toward the restrooms where, he hoped, he could find refuge.

He was almost there when a familiar figure appeared in front of him.

"You!" He cried out—and grabbed for the woman who had just emerged from her own refuge and was staring at him in horror.

***

That bastard Kelly has got Linda! Ms. Liu was kneeling alongside the metal doorframe, eyes locked on the scene at the back of the restaurant. He's got her!

She realized that she had to do something—anything—to help her partner get free. She could see that the gunfight was almost over. Any minute now the last of Jason's gang would either go down or give up.

What can I do? She asked herself. How can I get him to let her go?

A bullet struck near her, ricocheting away with an odd sound. She looked to that side, saw her bag lying there.

And had an idea.

***

Sean had realized what was happening as soon as Farrell came up from his seat with his gun out.

The rest of the gang is getting ready to shoot! He dropped to the floor and rolled behind the supine body of his erstwhile foe, thankful for the meager cover it gave him.

A moment later—he found out just how much he needed it.

Whoa! He ducked his head down low as bullets slammed into the floor all around him. They're not much for fire discipline!

172

He still had the gang leader's gun in his hand. It was, he thought, a Russian weapon.

I think it's a 454 Magnum Disposable, he looked the weapon over. I read about these somewhere—they're supposed to be really rare and not very accurate. Sean smiled. Let's see if those reports are right! He flicked the safety off and rolled free of his cover. One of the gangsters was less than ten feet from him, crouching behind a chair.

Sean fired three rounds at him.

Wow! Sean shook his head as he realized that not one of his shots had hit—despite the close range. In fact, he had missed so badly that his target hadn't even realized that Sean was shooting at him!

This thing is a piece of shit! Sean tossed it to one side and drew his own sidearm, clicking the safety off with a practiced motion and firing a single shot at the same target as soon as his sights lined up.

The man went down, clutching at a shattered shoulder.

One down, Sean shifted his aim to the right where another of the gangsters was hiding behind an overturned table. He waited until the man peered around the side of his cover, raising his pistol to take a shot at something.

Sean stroked the trigger of his 9-mil and nodded as the man went down. That's two. He looked for another target and saw nothing moving. I guess Frank got his pair. The thought that Kelly might have gotten one of the gunmen never crossed his mind. He made a final check of the room and, satisfied, started to get to his feet...

173

And dropped back down as a commotion broke out in the doorway.

Sean looked in that direction—and saw a slender figure stepping forward, an electronic remote of some kind in her hand.

That's Ms. Liu! He rolled back under cover and got up on one knee. What is she saying? The girl had been shouting in Chinese but now, as she saw that she had the attention of Sean and behind him, Farrell, she shifted to English.

"Put your guns down!" She brandished the remote with one hand and pointed toward the back of the room with the other. "Let my partner go or I will set off the explosives!"

Partner? Sean looked in the direction the girl was pointing and saw Kelly near the back of the room holding...

Is that Miss Lee? Sean had only seen the secretary once, but if that was her...

Of course! He nodded. We know that the two of them were working together on this. He smiled. They still think that the Claymore in the office is live! He flicked the safety 'OFF'. She has nothing to bargain with ...

An Asian man stepped in front of him. "Put the gun down," the man told him in perfect English. "We don't want her to kill us all!"

"You don't understand," Sean told him. "There is no explosive. We disarmed..."

The man lunged at Sean, grabbing for his pistol.

***

What the hell? Kelly stared at Ms. Liu who, in turn, was pointing at him as she shouted at the

174

crowd in Cantonese. She's going to set off an explosive? He frowned. What explosive?

The answer suddenly dawned on him.

Liu thinks the Claymore in the office is still live! He looked at Linda; saw the sudden confidence on her face. This one does too!

Kelly opened his mouth, ready to tell everyone in the restaurant the truth.

Just as one of the waiters leaped into him, dragging him away from his captive.

"No!" Kelly shook his head. "There is no explosive! We found it—disarmed it…"

The man paid no attention, just pushed Kelly back into the corner as he motioned for Linda to join her partner.

I can't let her get away, Kelly realized. I just can't! She's responsible for so many deaths…

He drew his pistol—and watched the waiter back away. "Get down," he told the man as he clicked the safety 'OFF', "I'll deal with you later," He turned and took aim at the fleeing back of his former secretary …

And squeezed the trigger.

CHAPTER NINETEEN

"NOOOOOOOO!" Ms. Liu screamed in agony as she saw Linda run toward her—then drop, lifelessly to the ground as Kelly fired his gun from behind her. "YOU BASTARD!" She held her remote up high and pressed the trigger just as hard as she could.

Nothing happened.

"We disarmed your explosive!" The older of the two recent arrivals yelled at her. "It won't go off!"

"Linda!" Liu took a half-step toward her partner. "Are you okay?"

Another shot rang out—a shot that just missed Ms. Liu and hit the Maître d' as he came up behind her. She looked up, saw Kelly aiming at her again, and realized what she had to do.

Before he could fire, she had turned and run out of the restaurant, quickly disappearing into the faceless throng that crowded the street.

***

"Why did you shoot her?" Farrell asked an hour later when the chaos in the restaurant had finally settled down and they'd been allowed to return to the office.

"Either Frank or I could have grabbed her," Sean told the CIA Chief. He'd been forced to fight off the waiter who'd grabbed for his gun and, as he wasn't sure exactly what was happening, he hadn't been any too gentle.

176

He hoped that the fingers he had broken would heal quickly.

"She was responsible for all those deaths," Kelly muttered, eyes on the floor. "Hell, because of her, I was at least partially responsible for them too!" He looked at Farrell. "I just couldn't let her get away once I had my hands on her."

"We're lucky that your friend, Inspector Lee showed up when he did." Farrell glanced at the bandage on his hand. "We nearly had an all-out riot!"

"He says that he can take care of it." Kelly shook his head. "Nobody in the restaurant was badly hurt and I promised that the Company would pay for the damages…"

"What is Ms. Liu going to do now?" Sean leaned forward, staring at the two older agents. "We killed her friend—her partner," he shook his head. "Hell, for all we know, her lover!" He slammed a hand down on the table. "What will she do to get revenge?"

"Almost anything." Farrell answered. "We know she has contacts in Hong Kong—the surviving gang-bangers told Inspector Lee that it was a call from her that brought them running to the restaurant."

"And she still has the rest of the paymaster information," Sean put in. "We know most of the Middle-East information is already in terrorist hands—what happens if she distributes the names of the people helping us in Russia? In China?"

"We have to find her." Farrell made a gesture. "As soon as we can."

"She can't get out of the country," Kelly said. "Inspector Lee has the air and sea-ports covered..."

"Against a computer whiz with who knows how many passports and a pile of money?" Sean snickered. "Fat chance of stopping her!"

"So what do we do?" Kelly held out his hands, his voice pleading.

"First we call Mary Max and tell her what just happened," Farrell looked at his watch. "She'll be in the office by now." He looked at Sean. "You're sure the secure phone line is safe?"

"I couldn't find anything physical and I'm sure there's no digital tap." He shrugged. "It's secure as far as I can tell."

"Good," he turned to Kelly. "You come with me while I report to Mary Max—she's gonna want to speak to you. You," he turned to Sean. "Get to work on the computer—call in whatever help you need from the FBI or NSA—see if you can find a way to locate the elusive Ms. Liu."

Sean nodded and headed for the desktop in Mrs. Lee's office.

"Now," Farrell looked at Kelly. "It's time for the two of us to face the music."

"The two of us?"

"Yeah," Farrell nodded, face angry. "I'm just as responsible for that circle-jerk in the restaurant as you are. I could have taken Ms. Liu down at any time but I didn't want to have to do it..."

"And you lost the shot when I took Linda down." Kelly nodded. "Just like old times in the sandbox."

"Yeah," Farrell nodded. "Except we don't have the resources we had there—and this cyber-warfare stuff is a lot harder to fight." He picked up the phone. "It's just eight in Washington," he dialed the number. "Let's see just how pissed off Mary Max is when we tell her how badly we screwed the pooch."

CHAPTER TWENTY

Victoria Liu was still staggering from reaction when she finally reached her efficient little apartment.

She's dead! He killed her! She had been replaying the scene in her mind's eye since fleeing from the restaurant. Linda had broken from Kelly's grasp, started to run toward the doorway where Liu waited …

She never got there. The burly Kelly drew his pistol and took careful aim at the fleeing woman's back …

Ms. Liu had stood, frozen in shock, as the American raised his gun and took aim. She had struggled to move, struggled to scream a warning…

It did no good. Linda wasn't paying attention; instead, her whole being was focused on running across the restaurant floor.

Running to join her partner.

Then that bastard from the CIA fired. Just one shot.

One deadly shot.

Liu had wailed in horror as she saw the bullet smash into her partner's back. The wail grew in volume as she watched her beloved stagger forward one step—two—then fall to the ground, her body limp, unmoving.

In that second Ms. Liu knew with total certainty that her friend, her partner, her lover, was dead.

I've got to get even with the bastard, she told herself as she fled. I've got to see him dead…

Her lips pulled back, baring her teeth. Even if I have to kill him with my own hands!

She began to make plans…

***

"So how do we find her?" Mary Max asked after listening to Farrell's report on what had happened in the restaurant. "By your report, I assume that it's the other one—this Ms. Liu—who has the data we're looking for. You didn't get it, did you?"

"No Ma'am," Farrell shook his head. "Linda—the dead girl—had nothing unusual on her."

"Have you checked her apartment?"

"We have," Kelly answered. "No one has lived there for some time."

"We're assuming that she's been living with Ms. Liu," Farrell added. "The evidence seems to indicate that they were a couple as well as a team."

"Is there any way to trace her cell phone?"

"I suspect that Ms. Liu discarded the cell phone she used to maintain contact with Mr. Kelly several days ago," Sean put in. "I found a burner cell in Ms. Chou's purse. I think it's safe to assume that Ms. Liu has one as well." He shrugged. "I'll try to activate the GPS tracker on the phone number we know, of course, but I doubt it'll come to anything."

"Wonderful." Mary Max's annoyance came through the secure line very clearly. "So after all this work, you have nothing at all."

"That's not exactly correct," Farrell put in. "We know the source of the leak. We know who has the information…"

181

"But you don't know where that information is located." Mary Max snarled. "Not much help to the people who are getting killed."

"Any more?" Sean asked. "My trace hasn't shown any."

"We're keeping the more recent killings quiet." There was a long pause. "I can tell you that there have been several additional deaths among those who helped us in the Middle East over the past twenty-four hours."

"Great," Farrell shook his head. "And now that we've killed her partner," he glared at Kelly. "There's no telling what Ms. Liu will do with the rest of the information."

"Perhaps she'll sell it to us." Mary Max put in. "In any case, the Secretary has authorized an attempt to purchase the data in question." She sighed. "Can you contact this 'Liu' woman?"

"Maybe," Sean ran his teeth over his lower lip as he thought about it. "I might be able to find her on the Deep Web…"

"Try it—try anything at all! You have to find that data before more of it finds its way into the wrong hands."

"We'll do our best, Ma'am." Sean nodded.

"You have to do better than that," her voice was stern. "You have to succeed."

There was the click of a receiver being replaced and the line went dead.

"So what do we do?" Kelly asked the other two men. "If I were her, I'd already be out of the country."

"You're not her," Farrell told him. "And I don't believe that she'll leave until she finds a way to get revenge."

"Revenge?"

"You killed her partner," Farrell leaned closer. "Hell, you shot her in the back! I'd say that was something that called for revenge."

"I didn't mean to kill her," Kelly shook his head. "That waiter dragged me away from her and by the time I got free of him…"

"What were you doing way in the back of the restaurant?" Sean asked eyes hard. "During a gunfight?"

"I…" Kelly's eyes flickered back and forth fearfully. "I thought I could get a better angle…"

"Bullshit!" Sean slapped his hand down on the table, the retort causing the CIA Station Chief to flinch back. "You were running away! You tried to get to the Men's Room to hide, didn't you?" Sean glared at him. "DIDN'T YOU?"

"YES! Yes," Kelly buried his face in his hands. "I was trying to get away." He looked into Sean's face. "Because I was scared! Afraid that I'd get hit. Afraid that I'd get shot…"

"So you ran away and left Sean and I to face four armed gang-bangers." Farrell shook his head. "You haven't changed, have you?"

"I guess not," Kelly almost whispered, eyes downcast. "I guess I haven't changed at all…"

"Come on, Sean." Farrell stood up and put a hand on his partner's shoulder. "We've got work to do." He headed for the door than looked back at the sobbing Station Chief. "Men's work…"

CHAPTER TWENTY-ONE

Kasim Rageah is dead; Ms. Liu discovered when she began checking on her contacts. Killed by Kelly and his people. She scrolled through her address book. Who else would be willing to help me take the bastard on? She flicked through name after name—finally stopping when one jumped out at her.

Muhammed Shaikh, she smiled bitterly. The Sword of India! They had tried to sell some of their information to Shaikh when they had first accumulated it. He refused us, she thought. Not because he didn't want the information, but simply because he couldn't afford our price.

That price had changed, she knew. If he was willing to help her do what she had to do…

He can have it all for free. She opened her browser and moved into the Deep Web. He can have anything I possess for the asking! She accessed his anonymous address and sent an e-mail. Let us see what he has to say to that offer…

***

In Des Moines, Iowa, Richard Klemensen stopped his car alongside his mailbox. It was raining out and he knew from long experience that the only way to avoid getting soaked was to lean out and grab his mail from the car.

He rolled down his window and reached out, opening the roadside door to the box…

The resulting blast blew out windows on both sides of the block. Bits of Klemensen's car were tossed nearly half a mile...

They never found any part of his body...

Mary Max was notified of Klemensen's death the next day. He had worked as an undercover source for the CIA for many years—but not in the Mideast. Klemensen had been a hotel manager in Malaysia—and had been a key force in a major Terrorist arrest just a few months prior.

April 15, Mary Max remembered. Tax day. Klemensen had found evidence that a number of militants were planning an attack on Kuala Lumpur. She frowned. He got that information to us in time to thwart the plot. She sighed. The Malaysian authorities arrested seventeen men, two of whom had trained with ISIS. She shook her head. Dick's name was kept out of every report on the event—and we pulled him back stateside afterwards. He did a good job—and the whole affair forced the Malaysian Government to introduce new anti-terror legislation.

She looked at the report on her desk. And now he's dead. She picked up her phone and dialed a number. His name got leaked—and there's only one place it could have come from. She turned to look out her window as the phone rang. My people have got to stop this now! Before we lose all our sources—and all our credibility!

***

"We lost another one," Farrell told Sean at breakfast an hour or so later. "Mary Max says he came from another region—not from the Mideast, but from Malaysia."

"More of the paymaster information is spreading," Sean sipped his coffee as he buttered some toast. "How upset is she?"

"Very." Farrell took some of his own coffee. "She knew this one—he was a friend."

"Great." Sean shook his head. "I did a little exploring in the Deep Web last night—I didn't come across any sign of the information we want." He took a bite of his toast. "I did put some feelers out—said I was looking for names of CIA spies in the Balkans."

"Think that'll work?"

"I don't know," Sean finished the toast, began buttering another piece. "It depends on just what Ms. Liu wants to do. If she's looking for funds to make a getaway, I'll hear from her. If not…"

"We've got to find other ways to locate her."

"There might be something we can use." Sean looked at his partner. "The remote detonator that Ms. Liu was waving around—did we get it after everything was cleaned up?"

"I don't know." Farrell pursed his lips. "I'd have to ask Kelly or Inspector Lee."

"Do that," Sean finished the last of his food. "We might be able to track the purchase."

"That's a thought." Farrell frowned as his partner signaled to the waitress. "I thought you were finished?"

"I'm still hungry." He ordered more toast, coffee, and another egg. "Remember, I never did get any dinner last night." He raised an eyebrow. "Or the night before. Or the night before that…"

"And you are a growing boy," Farrell grinned. "Just make sure you don't start growing horizontally!"

"Not a chance of that," Sean smiled. "Not with all the calories I burn and all the meals I miss on this job."

"Yeah," Farrell patted his own belly. "I know what you mean."

***

Ten minutes later, the two were walking into the offices of Universal Exports. "Kelly!" Farrell yelled as they opened the door to the Station Chief's office. "Do you know who got that remote thing Ms. Liu was waving around last night?"

"I think we have it," the burly CIA man opened a desk drawer, rattled around inside for a moment, then pulled it out. "Why? Do you have an idea?"

"Sean thinks it might have been purchased somewhere around here. If it was, there might be a record of the sale—and if Ms. Liu used a credit card…"

"We might be able to find an address!" Kelly smiled. "That's promising!" He stood and crossed his office, turning into the back area where his secretaries and analysts worked. "I'll have my girls look into it."

"Good," Farrell nodded, following alongside. "In the meantime, Sean is going to see what he can find on the Deep Web and you and I," he smiled. "Are going to see if we can find any connection between Kasim Rageah and either Linda or Liu."

"We'll get on it right away," Kelly handed the remote to a young woman, leaning down to explain what he wanted in Cantonese. She nodded and began examining the body of the device.

"Miss Ling will let us know if she finds anything. In the meantime, let's have a look at Linda's desk—we might find something there."

Farrell nodded and the two moved back to the front of the office. Linda's desk was the one closest to Kelly's and a quick examination showed that the drawers were locked.

"I'll get a screwdriver and we'll pry it open," Kelly said.

"Not so fast," Farrell bent closer, carefully examining the drawers. "Remember the claymore in the air vent—what if she left another surprise here…"

Kelly immediately took a long step back. "I hadn't thought of that." He looked at Farrell. "What do you think we should do?"

"Get the screwdriver," Farrell thought for a moment. "Along with a flashlight and some pliers." He looked into the burly man's face. "And this time, bring them right back—okay?"

"Just be a moment." Kelly turned and walked quickly to the back of the room. There was a closet in one wall and, when it was opened, Farrell could see normal office supplies—and a metallic tool kit.

"I'll bring the whole thing!" Kelly announced.

"Do that." Farrell began to run his fingers over the surface of the desk. "And tell the rest of the staff that now might be a good time to break for coffee."

Kelly nodded and spoke a few words of Cantonese. The secretaries stared at him for a second, than locked their desks, stood, and headed for the exterior door.

"Okay," Kelly put the toolbox down alongside the desk in question. "Now that they're out of here..."

"We can have a look." Farrell opened the box and pulled out a flashlight. "I hope your insurance is all paid up!"

CHAPTER TWENTY-TWO

Sean headed back to the secretaries area when he found no sign of Kelly or Farrell in the CIA Chief's office. He found them crouching in front of a desk, shining a light into the crack around the top drawer.

"What are you two doing?" Sean asked.

"You might want to go back outside," Farrell told him, squinting as he tried to make out anything touching both sides of the face of the desk drawer. "I think that Linda might have left a little present for us when she left." He got even closer, his forehead touching the desktop as he strained to see. "I'm trying to see…"

"Back off," Sean hurried to his partner's side. "Let me have a look." He bent down alongside the other man. "You know my eyesight is better than yours."

"Only because you're still a kid." Farrell backed up, rubbing the sweat which peppered his forehead. "Here," he handed Sean the penlight he'd been using. "Have a look."

"What am I looking for," the younger agent asked as he moved up close to the desk and pressed the light up tight against it.

"Anything unusual," Kelly, standing nervously on the far side of the desk said. "A bit of wire, some metal—anything touching both the drawer and the frame of the desk."

"Trigger mechanism," Sean smiled. "I understand." He squinted, eyeing the area in question. "Well," he moved the light down a little, changed the angle. "I don't see anything." He raised his head from the desk. "Besides, why would Linda do something to her desk? I'm sure she didn't know that we were going to find out what we did when we did."

"She called in sick…"

"Because she was selling the information they got—and probably planning to leave Hong Kong." Sean shook his head and shoved the head of the screwdriver into the drawer's lock, turning it hard. "She didn't have the time to set up a booby-trap in her desk!" He yanked the drawer open a few inches and shook his head sorrowfully as Kelly yelped and ducked down.

"You shouldn't have done that," Farrell told him sternly. "I'm the senior agent—you should have consulted with me first."

"I'm sorry, Frank. But it was obvious…"

"Not to me!" Farrell glared at the youngster. "I was the one who grew concerned over a possible booby trap! It wasn't your place…"

"Look," Sean held up a hand. "I'm sorry if I scared either one of you—but it's been a long couple of days and I really don't want to waste my time on 'possible' booby traps." He shook his head. "I promise that I'll never do it again, okay?"

"You'd better not!" Frank's eyes were still hard. "You're still a rookie at this—don't think you're not."

"Look!" Sean suddenly leaned down and looked into the drawer—on one side, just under the overhang of the desktop, sat something metallic. "That looks like…"

"It is," Farrell took the light from Sean's hand and shone it on the object. "That's a military fragmentation grenade."

"The pin's out!" Sean noted. "Spoon's held in place by the desktop…"

"What if you had pulled the drawer out all the way?" Farrell stared at his partner. "What do you think would have happened?"

"Crap." Sean shook his head. "I'm sorry, Frank. Really…"

"This time we all lucked out." Farrell's eyes held Sean's. "Next time, however…"

"There won't be a next time." Sean held up his hand, palm out, in a Boy Scout gesture. "I promise."

"Okay," Farrell smiled. "Now let's get that thing out and safe before something happens."

"And after we do," Sean put in. "Let's see what's in the desk that Linda felt was important enough to leave it behind as a guard."

***

Muhammed Shaikh was descended from a militiaman brought to China on a European ship. Like many before him, the young sepoy had married a Cantonese woman and set up shop in Hong Kong, doing laundry and tailoring for the Europeans that lived in the city.

That business had prospered and now, nearly a hundred years later, Muhammed Shaikh owned a number of such businesses spread throughout Hong Kong, Macau, and the Territories.

He had only one problem—Muhammed was a devout follower of Islam—and there were only six Mosques in Hong Kong—for more than 300,000

192

Muslims. A Mosque was under construction in the New Territories—but the land it sat on had taken years to acquire and Muhammed Shaikh was afraid of what might happen if more stories of ISIS and other such groups spread too widely amongst the local populace.

He had heard about the recent murder committed by Kasim Rageah but, as he did not consider the man a true Muslim, discounted its importance.

Despite that, he had to be prepared for trouble. Feelings about Muslim workers had grown mixed in recent days and if Islam was to spread through the East, it might become necessary to adopt some of the tenets of Jihad ...

Muhammed Shaikh knew that Jihad could be waged in many ways. Sometimes the discreet knife in the back was far more productive than the massed attack.

That was why he was interested in the information offered by Ms. Liu. If he could find out just who was working with the American Infidels in this part of the world, he might be able to protect his brothers in the difficult times that lay ahead.

And if he could sell some of those names to his brothers in Pakistan and Afghanistan, so much the better.

That was why he found himself standing in front of a small restaurant near Tsuen Wan station...

"Mr. Shaikh?" The voice was a bit hoarse, as if from a sore throat.

"I am Shaikh," Muhammed answered, turning to face the slim form behind him. "And you are..."

193

"My name is not important," Ms. Liu told him. "All you need know is that I am the one with the information that was discussed."

"All right," Muhammed nodded once. "I am here. You said that you were willing to reduce the price to something I would be pleased to offer?"

"I think so." Ms. Liu's face was hard, smudges around her eyes showing that she either hadn't slept or had been crying. "I only want one thing from you."

"Which is?"

"Not which," she held out her hand, showing him a piece of paper. "Who."

Muhammed Shaikh smiled and nodded as he looked at the paper.

"Deliver him to the address there," Ms. Liu told him. "And you will have all the names that we discussed."

"This man," Muhammed held up the paper. "Is he a government agent? If so, I would be reluctant…"

"He is an American," she told him. "And he has no official connection to the government of Hong Kong or that of China." She took a deep breath.

"Why do you want him?"

"He murdered my love," Ms. Liu almost sobbed the words. "I want vengeance!" She looked into Muhammed's eyes. "And I am willing to pay for it with information you will find invaluable to your cause."

"I understand," Muhammed Shaikh nodded, considering the task that lay ahead. "Yes," he nodded again. "I think we can do business."

194

"Good," Ms. Liu gestured toward the paper. "There is a cell phone number on that page—it will reach me no matter where I might be."

"Until I make that call then," Muhammed Shaikh smiled. "Farewell."

He turned and headed back to the train station. He had plans to make…

CHAPTER TWENTY-THREE

Brian Kelly grinned with relief as Frank Farrell tore a strip off his young partner. He'd come close to running when the younger man pulled the drawer open.

Now he was glad he'd managed to somehow stand his ground.

I really would have looked like a coward, he knew. It's bad enough as it is...

Kelly knew that he had a problem. Knew that he had become far too concerned—yes, say it--scared—when facing anything remotely resembling danger.

But I stood my ground while Frank checked out the desk, he told himself. Stayed with him and even handed him tools!

Even though his hands were shaking all the time.

It was a start, Kelly thought. A tiny step out of the darkness that's come to surround me.

He hoped the presence of his old friend would help him move further into the light.

"So," he asked when Farrell had finished. "What do we do now?"

"First we get this grenade out and safe." The older man turned to his partner. "Think you can get another of those rings?"

"If the collar hasn't been moved." He glanced at Kelly who shook his head. "Give me a minute."

"He's a smart kid." Kelly glanced back the way Sean had gone. "Way smarter than I was when I started."

"Smarter than me, too." Farrell nodded. "And you should see him shoot!"

"I've seen him fight," Kelly shook his head. "I wish I could do that kind of thing."

"So do I," Farrell looked the other man in the eye. "What's wrong with you, Brian?" He frowned. "Really?"

"Frank, I told you everything. I just..." He shook his head. "I just don't have it anymore. It seems like everything scares me."

"You should come in—see a doctor back in the World."

"Yeah," Kelly nodded. "Maybe." He grinned ruefully. "After you send in your report, I might not have any choice."

"I haven't decided what I'm going to say yet." Farrell studied his companion. "Maybe I..."

"Here!" Sean was suddenly back, a ring from the bondage collar in his hand. "This one should be heavy enough."

"Yeah," Farrell took it out of the youngster's hand. "That should be good." He leaned over the drawer. "I'm going to get my hand around the spoon on that grenade—when I have a good grip, I want you to slowly..." He looked at Sean. "And I do mean slowly—pull the drawer open."

"Got it." Sean moved into position. "Whenever you're ready."

"Okay," Farrell leaned over from the side of the desk, got his thumb on the spoon, cursed when it slipped off...

"Just a second…"

Kelly suddenly felt sweat begin to bead on his forehead. He might lose his grip, he thought. Might drop the grenade on the floor.

He found himself backing away.

It'll be safer down the hall, he told himself as he turned and speeded his retreat. I can keep an eye on the secretaries in my office. It's probably not safe to leave them alone…

Farrell looked up as the CIA man disappeared down the hall—and shook his head sadly.

***

"What did you find?" Kelly asked them a half-hour later.

"Not a whole lot," Farrell told him. "A few cryptic notes on the side of a pad that was in one of the drawers, a couple of bills, an old address book that might or might not give us something…"

"This," Sean held up the hand grenade. "Of course." He put it on Kelly's desk. "You'll note that it's an American grenade—and a fairly new one…"

"So?" Kelly's eyes were locked on the grenade—he couldn't pull them away.

"Where would she get a modern American grenade?" Sean asked. "I mean, it's not something you'd buy in a store anywhere in this part of town…"

"There are sources for such things." Kelly said, still staring at the green sphere. "Most are in Macau or the New Territories." He managed to turn his attention to the two agents. "I'll get someone working on it right away."

"Good," Farrell shook his head. "I still think we're missing something. Why would she set a booby trap like that unless there was something important in that desk?"

"Let me see the rest of the things you found," Kelly said, holding out his hand. "Maybe I'll see something you missed."

Farrell put the small sheaf of papers on the CIA Chief's desk. "I hope so, because I don't see..."

"Look at this!" Kelly's hand plunged into the pile and pulled out a bill. "Linda's apartment was in Kowloon but this bill..." He shuffled through the other papers, pulled out two more bills. "All of these are for an address in the New Territories!"

"Ms. Liu's apartment?" Sean suggested. "It would make sense if they were living together."

"Ms. Liu's apartment." Kelly nodded. "I think we have her."

"Let's move." Farrell told them. "Before another name and address gets into the wrong hands."

***

Ketut Jodog smiled as he looked at his own handiwork.

This is coming out well, he thought. I never thought of doing this kind of carving before but the money is good so why not?

He glanced at the photos he was using as reference. I never even heard of Velociraptors before, he smiled. Although my son tells me that they are very famous because of an American Film.

The carving was going to an American company—as were several others he had already completed.

199

All Dinosaurs, he shook his head again. Things of the past!

Ketut thought of his own past for a long moment.

He had been an important man once—an official at the Ngurah Rai International airport...

Perhaps I should never have spoken of the things I saw. Perhaps I should have stayed silent, allowed the bomb to explode—it would not have harmed me.

He knew, however, that it would have harmed hundreds of others—all of them innocent tourists on vacation.

I couldn't let it happen.

Ketut had called a number he had been given by a government official—it did not, however, put him in touch with anyone in his own government, instead, it was answered by a man who spoke with an American accent.

I still do not know who he was, Ketut thought. But he sent men who quickly found and disarmed the explosive.

Later, those same men had raided a stronghold of Jemaah Islamiyah—the group who had planted the bomb. Several of their members were killed in the fight—others went to jail.

Ketut ran his hand down the dinosaur's flanks. I was given a reward for my aid. Enough money to start my own business. He looked around his little shop. So why am I so worried?

He had read—on the ISIS website—about several men who had been 'punished' for helping the American Infidels against the chosen of Allah.

When I took my reward, I was told that no one would ever know of it—that my association with the American CIA would forever be a secret. He remembered the names on the ISIS site. I wonder if those men were told the same thing? He caressed the dinosaur once more. I wonder…

The doorbell rang.

Look at me! Ketut had jumped at the sound of the bell. I am acting like a little child afraid of spirits! He put the dinosaur down and strode to the door. Why should I be afraid in my own house? Who would hurt me…?

He opened the door. A man stood directly in front of him, a pistol in his hand.

"You are Ketut Jodog?"

Ketut could do nothing but nod silently.

"You have betrayed your brothers in Allah." The gun came up, leveled in front of Ketut's face. "You are a traitor to your faith—your people."

The man clicked the safety on his weapon 'OFF'.

"You must die."

Ketut stared into the dark hole of the weapon's barrel—a hole that suddenly burned as bright as the sun—as Ketut's world went forever dark.

CHAPTER TWENTY-FOUR

"Do you think this is the place?"

Sean, Farrell, and Kelly had taken the Metro (Kelly had not yet replaced the silver van) to the station nearest the address they had found.

"I mean, it doesn't look like much…"

Tsuen Wan station was very near the coast. The main flightpath out of Hong Kong International airport went directly overhead and planes went over with deafening regularity.

"The address on this bill is right over there," Kelly pointed to an apartment building across the street from the station. "Let's have a look."

"Carefully." Farrell put in. "Remember the grenade hidden in the office desk."

"Yeah," Sean nodded. "If nobody answers the door…"

"We check for booby-traps before we enter." Farrell looked at his two companions. "Everybody clear on that?"

"I'm certainly not going to kick in the door," Kelly told them. "I'm too old and too stiff for that!"

"I won't do anything without your permission, Frank." Sean added.

"Okay," Farrell gestured for them to follow him. "Let's go and take a look."

The address on the bill led them to the rear of the apartment building's third floor.

"Kelly," Farrell directed Sean to the other side of the door. "You speak the language."

"Lucky me." The burly CIA man took a deep breath and knocked—rather gingerly—on the door.

Nothing happened.

"Harder!" Farrell whispered from his place on the left. "If they have a radio or TV on…"

Kelly knocked again. More forcefully this time—and slid to his left as he did so.

Again, nothing happened.

"I guess there's no one home." Farrell moved past Kelly and pulled a flashlight out of his pocket. "Sean—check the other side."

The younger agent nodded and, with his own flashlight, carefully studied the space between the door and the frame.

"I don't see anything unusual." He finally announced.

"Nor do I," Farrell responded. "Just stand by for a second…"

The older agent examined the lock and doorknob and pulled a small device out of his pocket.

"The lock isn't new," he opened the device up, showing it to be a lock pick. "Let's see…"

He inserted the pick into the lock and manipulated it, feeling around for the tumblers until…

CLICK!

The lock opened.

"Carefully now," Farrell pushed the door open…

And exhaled. "Okay, it doesn't look as if this place is booby-trapped," he stepped inside, running the beam of his flashlight over the interior. "Come on, let's check it out."

Sean followed immediately, his own light running over the entryway. Kelly hesitated for a long moment—then stepped inside behind them.

"Light switch over here," Sean noted. "Should I turn it on?"

"Go ahead," Farrell shrugged. "We can't be afraid of everything!"

Sean clicked the switch down and smiled as both a ceiling fixture and a desk lamp came on.

"Not a very big place," he pointed out. "I assume that the door there leads to the toilet and the one over there," he nodded to his right. "Goes to the bedroom."

"You're probably right." Farrell took another step forward. "Kelly and I will check those out, I want you..." He pointed to the desk in front of the back wall and the laptop sitting on top of it. "To check out that computer."

"On it."

"Captain?" Farrell gestured to the two doors.

"I asked you not to call me that," the burly CIA chief headed for the right hand door. "And I'll take the bedroom."

"Of course you will," Farrell headed for the second door, making a cursory check of the knob before opening it.

The bathroom was quite utilitarian, with none of the feminine touches he would have expected to find in a similar apartment back in the states. "Nothing obvious," he called out. "I'm gonna have to look around for a moment."

He lifted the cover on the toilet, searching for anything that might be hidden.

And found nothing.

"Room's clean," he told Sean who was still working on the computer. "Nothing in there to help us."

"This is definitely Ms. Liu's apartment," the other agent told him.

"How do you know?"

"Her passport is here," he held up the blue booklet. "Linda's too."

"So she's still in the country," Kelly said as he re-entered from the bedroom. "Anything in the computer?"

"It's password protected." Sean shrugged. "I can get in by brute force but I'm afraid that it would destroy any data if I did so."

"Take it back to the office," Kelly told him. "Fiddle with it there." The CIA man looked around. "Take the passports too." He frowned. "I feel very uncomfortable out here…"

"I know what you mean," Farrell nodded. "It's almost like being out in the field, isn't it?"

"Let's go," Kelly waved an arm. "I'll get surveillance on this apartment. If Ms. Liu comes back, we'll pick her up."

"I hope it happens soon," Farrell shook his head. "I have a really bad feeling about this whole situation."

"You always have 'bad feelings'," Kelly told him as they exited the apartment building and headed for the train station. "You had them in Iraq; you had them in Afghanistan…"

Farrell shrugged.

A moment later, they were on the platform waiting for the next train back to the office.

Nobody noticed the slender girl watching them from the opposite side of the tracks…

***

Bastards found my apartment! Ms. Liu watched while the three Americans boarded the train and started the trek back to their office. They will have taken my laptop, she sighed. And my passport.

Liu shrugged. It doesn't matter. They can't get anything out of my computer and I don't need the passport. She watched the train disappear into the distance. I'm not leaving until I'm done with Mr. Kelly…

She took one of her burner phones out of her bag and dialed a number.

"Mr. Shaikh?" She said as someone answered on the other end. "Have you made a decision?" She listened. "Good." A smile appeared on her face. "I can tell you where he is right this moment." She looked down the tracks. "He's on a train bound for the City Center." She rubbed a bit of dust from beneath her eye. "He'll be back in his office within the hour." She listened again. "Tonight?" She nodded. "Good, I will expect to hear from you before morning."

She clicked her phone off and smiled, then headed for the stairs to the street and her apartment building.

I have a little time before they get someone out here to watch my apartment. She hurried across the street. I'll get what I need and find someplace else to stay until Mr. Shaikh gives me what I want. She smiled. After that, I don't really care …

***

"Security on this thing is really tight," Sean muttered an hour or so later. "It's going to take a while for me to make any real progress."

"Leave it until later," Farrell told him. "You haven't gotten much rest in the past few nights."

"I'm okay," Sean rubbed at the stubble on his cheeks. "I'll stay and put in a couple of hours."

"Okay," Farrell turned to Kelly. "I'll stick with him for a while—we'll order some food." He smiled. "I feel safer eating here than in any of the restaurants in this area."

"I'm going to head back to my place." Kelly yawned and stretched. "I need a couple of hours sleep."

"See you here in the morning." Farrell waved. "Sleep well."

"I plan to." Kelly headed for the door. "Lock up when you leave."

Then he was gone.

"I can't figure that guy out," Sean told his partner. "Sometimes he's perfectly normal—like he was just then. Other times…"

"His nerve's gone," Farrell frowned toward the door. "It happens to a lot of men if they've been in the field too long. He needs a rest," he shrugged. "And a little professional help."

"If you say so," Sean looked at his partner. "I thought I heard dinner mentioned?"

"I'll call out." He produced a folded menu from a pocket. "That place that Bruce suggested okay with you?"

"Fine," Sean smiled. "Just stay away from the Szechuan stuff—it's a little too hot for me!"

"Okay," Farrell dialed the number on the menu. "Sissy!"

***

Outside, Brian Kelly started to cross the street than hesitated. Do I really want to let them work on this alone—without me? He turned and looked at the lights in the office of Universal Exports. I know Farrell is going to submit a report on me—he's going to have to. He licked dry lips. Do I want to give him more ammunition?

He stood there for a long moment, wondering what would be the best thing to do.

The decision was taken out of his hands when a car roared to a stop in front of him and he felt the muzzle of a pistol dig into the small of his back.

"Come with us, Mr. Kelly," a voice said in badly accented Cantonese. "Our boss wants to talk to you."

A moment later Kelly was in the back seat of the car, squeezed between two men, one of whom held a pistol where he could see it.

"Sit back," the man with the gun told him. "Be comfortable." He smiled showing bad teeth and emitting equally bad breath. "It's going to be a long ride!"

The car pulled away and headed away from the city.

CHAPTER TWENTY-FIVE

"You have him?" Ms. Liu's face lit up. "Where?" She nodded. "All right, I will wait until morning—it will be safer for all of us that way." She grinned. "Just don't break him until I get there."

She hung up and stared out of her room's window. They have him, she thought. And tomorrow it will be my turn. She smiled. Although I won't keep him for very long…

She began to prepare for bed—although she was sure she wouldn't be sleeping.

***

"All right," Sean smiled at what he saw on the monitor. "I think I might have it!"

"What do you have?" Farrell yawned, sitting up straighter in his chair. "Something useful, I hope."

"I think so." Sean opened up a file, studied it for a second, opened a second. "Yeah, I think this is just what we've been looking for!"

"Show me!"

"See this file?" Sean opened one of several now visible on the laptop. "This is the paymaster file that was hacked from the CIA." He quickly scrolled through it. "It's broken down by area…" He enlarged a page, showed it to Farrell. "And you can see that this one's been marked as 'SOLD'."

"So you found the paymaster file." Farrell shrugged. "I think the CIA already has a copy of that."

"Yeah," Sean opened the second file. "But they don't have a copy of this!" He looked at his partner. "Yet."

"What is it?" Farrell leaned closer. "Looks like another bunch of names…"

"These are the buyers that Liu and Lee found." He pointed at the dollar figures underneath. "And this is what they paid for the data."

"Mary Max is going to want a copy of that!" Farrell smiled and glanced at his watch. "Six o'clock." He shook his head. "Doesn't matter-- she's going to want it enough that she won't complain when I wake her up!"

He reached for the phone and dialed her number.

She didn't complain: "You have all of the buyers?" Mary Max had come instantly awake when Farrell told her the news. "And the names they got?"

"Every one of them, Ma'am." Sean told her. "I've already sent it to your computer in a coded packet."

"We can put guards on the ones that are in jeopardy," Mary Max muttered. "And track down the buyers…" She realized she was still on the phone. "Can we track the buyers?"

"There are e-mail addresses," Sean replied. "Most are in the Deep Web but it shouldn't be too hard to track them down." He smiled. "I'm sure the FBI Cyber team could do it in no time!"

"This is wonderful," she told them. "You've done a magnificent job!"

"We're not done yet," Farrell told her. "The actual hacker is still on the loose."

"I'm sure you'll find her." Mary Max's voice told them just how happy she was. "Stay until you do."

"Yes Ma'am."

"Now tell me about Mr. Kelly." Her voice sharpened as she spoke the CIA Station Chief's name. "Has he been useful?"

"He's done his share, Ma'am." Farrell said, eyes on his partner. "He has some problems…"

"So I gathered." Mary Max paused to think. "Should I arrange for his recall?"

"It would be better if he came in on his own," Farrell sighed. "I think I can convince him that would be the right thing to do."

"If you can't," her voice was sharp now. "I will bring him in without his consent—you understand?"

"Yes Ma'am." Farrell nodded. "I'll take care of it."

"Good." The two agents could hear their boss barely suppress a yawn. "Call me again later today; I'll let you know how things are going at this end." She hesitated, then: "And please, don't call until after noon my time!"

"Yes Ma'am," Farrell grinned. "We just thought that this was too important to wait."

"It was," they could hear another yawn. "It was—but don't make a habit of waking me up, all right?"

"Yes Ma'am." Farrell gave Sean a look. "We'll speak to you later today—after the noon hour your time."

"Good." Mary Max yawned again. "Good night—and don't forget what I said about Kelly."

211

They heard her hang up.

"Can we get some sleep now?" Farrell asked. "Or do you have anything else you want to do?"

"No," Sean stood up and stretched. "I can take a break."

"Good, because…"

"Mr. Farrell!" Bruce Lee pushed the door open. "Where's Mr. Kelly?"

"He left a few hours ago," Farrell frowned. "Why?"

"No one came to relieve me at Ms. Liu's apartment—I had to call another agent to take my place." He looked at Farrell. "After I tried and failed to reach Mr. Kelly."

"You couldn't get him?"

"There has been no answer on his cell," Bruce shook his head. "After Hong reached the apartment and relieved me, I went to Mr. Kelly's apartment." He looked from Farrell to Sean. "He wasn't there and his bed had not been slept in."

"Maybe he just went to dinner."

"No," Bruce shook his head again. "I know his favorite restaurants. He has not been to any of them."

"Bars?"

"Mr. Kelly does not drink."

"Then what…"

"She got him," Sean suddenly realized. "Ms. Liu—she grabbed Kelly."

"Why would she do…" Farrell suddenly nodded. "He shot her lover."

"And now she wants revenge." Sean closed the captured laptop and opened his own machine.

"We've got to find him before she gets what she wants."

But how?"

"If he's still got his phone, I can track it." Sean brought up the proper programs, stared at the results. "It's turned off right now but I can use the local towers to switch it on." He tapped in a series of commands. "That should do…" He leaned in closer. "There!" He pulled up a map of cell towers, ran a trace program. "He's in the Territories…" He ran a second program. "Somewhere near Lo Wu station."

"Can you get it any closer than that?"

"It'll take a few minutes…"

"Do it," Bruce Lee told him. "While you do, I will arrange transportation." He smiled. "My father will want to be there when we capture this woman who caused my mother's death."

"Okay," Sean settled in to work. "Give me fifteen minutes."

"Make it ten," Farrell told him, studying the map he'd called up on his phone… "It's a long way from here and I don't think Kelly would appreciate our being late."

***

Kelly was, at that very moment, sitting in a metal chair in near-total darkness, his hands cuffed behind him.

I'm somewhere near the water, he knew, having seen docks as the car that had taken him away from the city drove through the open doors of what appeared to be a warehouse. They didn't take my phone, maybe…

A door opened, flooding the interior of Kelly's room with light.

"Mr. Kelly," the voice was hoarse, as if its owner had been drinking—or crying. "So good of you to come."

Kelly turned toward the voice.

"I never knew what Linda saw in you," Ms. Liu stalked into the room. "I mean, you're a big man..." She smiled a bitter smile. "But size isn't everything, is it?"

"What..." Kelly licked suddenly dry lips. "What do you want with me?"

"You shot my Linda." Ms. Liu was closer now. "Shot her in the back!" She stopped directly in front of him. "What do you think I want from you?"

"No," Kelly shook his head. "Please, you don't understand..."

"I understand all too well." Ms. Liu's eyes held those of the CIA Chief. "She was about to get away from you."

She inched closer.

"You couldn't allow that."

Closer still.

"So you shot her."

They were nearly eye to eye now.

"You shot her so she couldn't reveal what kind of man you really are. A man who would chain a woman to his bed. Gag her with rubber and leather..."

"She liked that!"

"No," Ms. Liu shook her head. "She put up with it. Put up with it because she loved you!"

"Then why..."

214

"Why did she leave you?" Ms. Liu's voice was soft now—Kelly had to strain to hear it. "She left because she could no longer watch while you played your little games with the other women in your office. With Mrs. Lee and Ms. Ting…"

"I never touched them!"

"You wanted to!" Ms. Liu spat the words out. "Even while you were making love to Linda, you were thinking about the next woman on your bed. And the next. And the next…" Ms. Liu sighed. "She and I were friends for a long time and she finally came to me for help getting away from you." She glared at the big man. "I was happy to help her…"

"You did more than that!" Kelly growled.

"Yes," Ms. Liu nodded. "I loved her." Her eyes hardened. "And you killed her." She smiled a crooked smile. "And now it's my turn."

Ms. Liu turned and signaled someone in the other room.

Brian Kelly began to shiver in fear.

215

CHAPTER TWENTY-SIX

"He's up that way," Sean looked at his laptop. "Somewhere above the water."

"There are a number of warehouses in that area," Inspector Lee noted as he scrolled through the data on his tablet. "A few are deserted and waiting for new tenants."

"He's gotta be in one of them," Sean nodded. "About two thirds of the way down the street I think."

"The next few buildings are owned by a man named 'Muhammed Shaikh', the Inspector turned to Farrell. "He is huihui!"

"What does that mean?"

"According to my sources," Sean had opened another window to check the term, "it comes from the time of the Yuan Dynasty when large numbers of Muslims came from the west." He looked at Inspector Lee. "The land of the Uyghurs, who the Chinese called the 'Hui People' were in the west, it became common to call foreigners of all religions, including Muslims, "HuiHui"."

"And Mr. Shaikh is Muslim?"

"His family has been here for many years." The Inspector checked his own files. "They have always been Muslims." He turned to Farrell. "Mr. Shaikh is well-respected in his community."

"But I'll bet he's getting some heat from the fundamentalists." Farrell stroked his chin. "I wonder what he would give for some of the data

Ms. Liu has been selling to his co-religionists all over the world."

"The use of his warehouse for one thing." Sean turned his laptop screen around so the others could see it. "Kelly's phone is definitely inside."

"All right," Bruce Lee pulled the car over to the curb across from the warehouse in question. "Let us see if you are right."

The four men quickly crossed the street. At Farrell's suggestion, Bruce and Sean were to make their entrance from the rear of the warehouse while he and the Inspector entered from the front.

"Signal when you're in position," Farrell told his partner.

"How?" Sean asked, looking down the length of the building.

"Send a text—we'll go five seconds later."

"Okay," the younger agent nodded and motioned for the tall Asian to follow him.

"What do you really expect to find inside?" The Inspector asked.

"I'm not sure," Farrell shrugged. "I believe Sean when he tells me that Kelly's phone is inside."

"You think it's a trap?"

"Why?" Farrell spread his hands. "What could Ms. Liu possibly gain by…?"

His phone chirped, indicating a test was incoming. "Okay," he drew his handgun and jacked a round into the chamber. "Five seconds…" Farrell stepped to the door.

"Four…"

He silently turned the knob.

"Three…"

And pushed the door forward just enough to keep it from locking.

"Two..."

Farrell clicked the safety on his gun to 'OFF' and...

"ONE!"

Pushed the door inward with his body pressed tight against it, his eyes searching for a target.

There was nothing in sight.

"Okay," he looked at Inspector Lee who had moved to his left. "There're two doors on the far wall, one of them will lead to an office, the other..."

His phone chimed again. This time Farrell looked at the text. "Through the right hand door," he shoved the phone back into his pocket. "Hurry!"

The right hand door led into the warehouse proper. There were long lines of shelving on both walls—all of them empty. A car sat near the back of the building and, right in front of it, there was a metal chair.

Brian Kelly was in that chair.

He wasn't alone. Ms. Liu stood at his side, she had been looking at the car but now, alerted by the sound of the door opening, she turned to face Farrell and the Inspector.

"Come in, Gentlemen." She motioned toward the car. "Join your friends."

Farrell saw Sean rise up a little from his position behind the car. "Be careful, Frank." He gestured toward the girl. "She has an explosive vest!"

"So does your Mr. Kelly!" The girl added. "Does that mean you will leave now?"

"Don't do anything foolish, Ms. Liu." Farrell called out. "There's no reason for anyone to get hurt."

"There was no reason for my Linda to get hurt!" Ms. Liu gestured toward Kelly. "That was his work—and today, he's going to pay for it."

"Settle down," Farrell saw Sean drawing a bead on the back of the woman's head—and waved him off. "Let's talk about this."

"Talk?" Ms. Liu sneered. "I thought you Americans were 'Men of Action!'." She shook her head. "Have you all become as bloodless as your so-correct President?"

Farrell holstered his pistol and took a long step forward.

"There's no need for action here." He took another step. "We found your list of clients—they can't help you anymore."

"I don't care about that," Ms. Liu spat. "The sale of names—that was Linda's work—a way for us to raise enough money to leave this place and have a good life together." She looked at the still form of Kelly. "If it hadn't been for him, we'd already be gone!"

"I understand." Farrell had closed to within fifteen feet, the inspector moving along beside him. "But the names you sold were people—real people like you and..." He looked at her, calculating. "And like Linda." He shook his head. "Some of them are dead—murdered..."

"I don't care." She held up her hand and, for the first time, Farrell could see the flat plastic device she was holding. "All I care about is getting the revenge my Linda deserves." She smiled. "This detonator will guarantee that!"

"Ms. Liu…" Farrell saw Sean begin to move from behind the girl, working silently across the concrete floor in her direction. "There must be another way."

"No!" She suddenly shouted, raising her hand high. "And if your friend doesn't get back…"

"Go ahead back, Sean." Farrell motioned with his hand. "We don't want to antagonize the lady."

"Lady!" Ms. Liu spat the word. "What do you know about ladies?" She glanced at Kelly. "Linda was a lady—and this one put a collar on her and treated her like an animal!"

"Mr. Kelly has a problem," Farrell held his hands in front of him. "I promise you that he'll get help…"

"You think that you can help him!" She suddenly grinned widely. "I will give you the chance." She backed away, the remote still held tightly in her hand. "Go ahead—see if you can free him, but I warn you, if you make the slightest mistake…"

She made an explosive gesture with her hands.

Farrell nodded and hurried to Kelly's side, scanning the explosive vest fastened to his chest and waist as he came.

"Hey," He smiled at his old associate. "You really got yourself into one this time."

"You and the others should clear out," Kelly was sweating despite the cool interior of the warehouse. "This vest has a radio detonator—she can set it off whenever she wants!"

"How is it attached?"

"There's a buckle behind my back." Kelly shook his head. "I don't think she'll let you get to it."

"Neither do I." Farrell turned to Ms. Liu. "Can my partner join me?"

"Why not?" She answered.

Sean was at Farrell's side before she had finished speaking.

"Can you block the frequency of her detonator?" The older agent asked.

"Not a chance," Sean shook his head. "I don't have the equipment I would need to block that many frequencies and I have no way to find which one she's on." He shrugged. "Sorry."

"It's okay," Farrell turned back to the vest. "Do you see any kind of booby traps on this thing?"

"You're more of an expert than I am," Sean bent closer, scanned the front of the vest. "There!" He nodded at an inch-long cylinder made of clear plastic. "That could be a Tremblor switch..."

"Probably is." Farrell took a closer look. "It's pretty coarse—it would take more than a gentle movement..."

"It will go off if I try to run," Kelly told them, a slight stammer to his voice. "She warned me about that."

"We could shoot her—if I had a clear shot, I could take her down before she could push the button..."

"What if it's a dead man's switch?" Farrell asked. "What if she's already pressed it and only the pressure of her finger is stopping this from going off."

"I hadn't thought about that..."

221

Farrell sighed. "I don't know…"

"You can't leave me here, Frank." Kelly looked at him pleadingly. "You can't let her kill me!"

"We won't, Captain." Farrell smiled. "Don't worry."

"Don't call me that," Kelly whispered. "Please…"

"Come on," Farrell stood up and motioned for Sean to join him. "Let's see if we can talk some sense into the girl." He shook his head. "And failing that, let's see if we can figure a way to get the detonator away from her." He looked at Kelly. "Without setting anything off!"

The two of them walked away from the CIA chief, eyes on the slender form of Ms. Liu.

CHAPTER TWENTY-SEVEN

She's not going to listen to them, Kelly thought as he watched the two men walk away. She's going to kill me no matter what it costs her.

I'm going to die.

Kelly had known the truth for some time—but he had fooled himself into believing that the other two agents would find a way to free him—a way to disarm the explosives.

Now he knew that was not going to happen.

They're going to die too, he realized. Farrell won't leave me here—he'll try something and when the explosives go off, he'll be killed. He looked at the two men with eyes suddenly opened to the reality of the situation. The kid too—he won't leave either, he'll die right alongside his partner.

Kelly shook his head. I let his father die—I can't be responsible for the son's death too!

I just can't!

Brian Kelly began to think—and as he did, the fear slowly faded away, replaced by calm acceptance—and a resurgence of courage lost many years before.

***

"She won't budge," Farrell said as he and Sean re-joined the Inspector and Bruce Lee. "She's determined to kill both Kelly and herself." He looked at his companions. "But there's no reason for us to die as well."

"You're sure there's nothing we can do?" Inspector Lee's eyes moved to Ms. Liu and the hand that held the detonator. "Can't we just shoot her?"

"That detonator she's holding is a dead man's switch," Farrell told him. "I had a look at it—it'll go off if her hand relaxes." He shook his head. "There's just no way to stop her from setting it off."

"Maybe we could grab her hand," Bruce put in. "Knock her down..."

"She won't let any of us get close enough." Farrell looked the tall Asian in the eye. "You have to get out of here." He gestured at the Inspector. "Both of you."

"How about you?"

"I'm going to try one more thing," Farrell looked into Inspector Lee's eyes. "It's dangerous, but..."

"I understand." Inspector Lee smiled and offered his hand. "It's been an honor to work with you."

"And with you," Farrell grasped the offered hand. "I hope you'll work as closely with the new Station Chief as you have with Mr. Kelly."

"And I hope he will be more worthy of your help," Sean put in.

"Thank you," Inspector Lee nodded. "I'm sure he will be." He patted Bruce on the shoulder and the two of them headed for the front door.

"You're going with them," Farrell told his partner. "Right now."

"Not a chance,' Sean replied. "I'm not going to leave my partner in a situation like this."

"Sean..."

"Listen, Frank. I don't know what you have in mind but whatever it is," Sean shrugged. "It'll have a better chance of success with the two of us working together."

"I don't..."

"It's time!" Ms. Liu's voice cut through the argument between the partners. "Leave now—it is your last chance."

"Ms. Liu," Sean turned toward her. "What if..."

"No!" She backed away from Sean, her back to Kelly. "No more talk! I am going to count to thirty—if you are not on your way out, I will not hesitate to set off both the explosive belts." She kept moving backward. "One...Two...Three...Four..."

Behind her, Brian Kelly was coming to his feet with infinite care, his eyes locked on Ms. Liu's back.

"Look!" Sean whispered into Farrell's ear."

"I know," the older agent returned. "Don't tip it off."

"Five...Six...Seven..."

Kelly came completely upright and took a last long look at Farrell and Sean, then: "GET DOWN!" He yelled as loud as he could.

Ms. Liu turned toward him, eyes wide.

And Brian Kelly jumped on top of her just as she released her 'Dead Man's Switch'.

CHAPTER TWENTY-EIGHT

"I didn't think he had the nerve," Sean muttered as he slowly pushed himself upright. There was a hole in the concrete floor of the warehouse some thirty feet in front of him—half covered by scraps of iron and aluminum from the ceiling and surrounding shelves.

"He used to be a good man," Farrell told him, pulling out a splinter of metal that had lodged in his forehead. "At the end, he finally got his nerve back." The older man shook his head. "He knew that most of the power of one of those belts goes forward, that's why he jumped on top of her…"

"So what do we do now?"

"We let Mary Max know what's happened here," Farrell groaned as he rose, rubbing a sore spot where his knee had slammed into the concrete. "Then we find Muhammed Shaikh and make sure his copy of the paybook is off the streets." He smiled. "Then we go home!"

"Home." Sean shook his head. "I guess I should call my mother and tell her what's been going on."

"I wouldn't mention Brian Kelly," Farrell shook his head. "She's not too fond of him."

"Yeah, I get that." Sean looked at the carnage where Kelly had leaped on top of his captor. "But he did come through in the end."

"He did that." Farrell put a hand on his partner's shoulder. "Come on; let's get out of this place before the rest of the roof collapses."

"Yes sir," Sean smiled. "I'm all for that, sir."

Together, they walked out of the warehouse and into the light of the Hong Kong sun, their mission complete, their work done.

For now...

THE END